Something fell from the sky.

A shadow blasted across the truck, briefly barricading the sun. An instant later, a machine of wood and twanging wires flew across the truck's hood, missing it by the breadth of a hand. Smoke coiled out behind it. The howling contraption flipped in the air, bits of it snapping free even as it dropped, and then it struck a patch of wild forget-me-nots on the side of the road, crushed them, and vanished in the tall grass beyond.

Ellenor torqued the steering wheel to the right and applied brake and clutch, her breath trapped behind her teeth. The truck came to a jarring halt, the two white brood boxes sliding in the back and dislodging a hundred dead bees. Exhaling, she looked from the window in the direction of whatever the hell it was. The war rarely reached this far from the Front; she never fell asleep with the sound of German artillery pounding French hillsides, as so many others did. Other than the occasional supply convoy from the factories in Berlin, Father's estate and the villages nearby saw no evidence of the blood being hemorrhaged by millions a few dozen miles away. But Ellenor knew, staring from the truck's dusty window, a part of the war had almost crushed her. Its smoke rose like a serpent from where it waited in the grass.

She opened the door.

Praise for Lance Hawvermale

"Deftly written, [Hawvermale's] debut is full of appealing characters and moments that sparkle with tenderness."

~Publisher's Weekly

~*~

"In a medium that is saturated with go-to potboilers, Lance Hawvermale's novel shines above it, with vibrant writing and exhilarating flair."

~Criminal Element

~*~

"[Hawvermale] pushes the envelope, taking the commonplace theme of women's friendships into dangerous territory and dramatizing what women can do not just to help themselves, but also to bring justice to others."

~Booklist

~*~

"Hawvermale, balancing suspense with character study, includes enough pauses between the adrenaline-pumping scenes to give his leads the time they need to grow."

~Kirkus Reviews

~*~

"Hawvermale expertly weaves complex characters and secrets, luring you from one chapter to the next. His prose is at the same time smooth and riveting, and his detective will stay with you even after you've closed the back cover."

~Jean Rabe, author

The Beekeeper's Bullet

by

Lance Hawvermale

Wind in the Wire, Book 1

This is a work of fiction. Names, characters, places, and incidents are either the product of the author's imagination or are used fictitiously, and any resemblance to actual persons living or dead, business establishments, events, or locales, is entirely coincidental.

The Beekeeper's Bullet

Cover Art by *Tina Lynn Stout*

The Wild Rose Press, Inc.
PO Box 708
Adams Basin, NY 14410-0708
Visit us at www.thewildrosepress.com

Publishing History
First Vintage Rose Edition, 2019
Print ISBN 978-1-5092-2751-8
Digital ISBN 978-1-5092-2752-5

Wind in the Wire, Book 1
Published in the United States of America

Dedication

To Jerry, Kathy, and Beth

"Once you have tasted flight, you will forever walk the earth with your eyes turned skyward, for there you have been, and there you will always long to return."

~*Leonardo da Vinci*

Part One
The Flight

Lance Hawvermale

Chapter One

She drove down from the mountain, the dead colony in the back of Father's truck. He wasn't her *real* father, of course. But his house was grand and his command of Brahms on the piano even grander, and the only people who didn't call him Father were those who smoked Turkish tobacco with him in the parlor. And Ellenor Jantz may have been quite brash for a woman of 1917, but her moxie stopped just short of cigars.

The truck bucked through holes in the German countryside, its joints creaking. She tried not to think about the bees.

Instead of bees: mathematics. Her two young charges—Father's children, ages seven and ten—preferred penmanship and English-language studies over their multiplication tables, but today was Tuesday, and Tuesday meant math. Ellenor herself was no Pythagoras when it came to such things, but she'd been hired over three other quite capable tutors because she was American, she was adept at all things academic, and she could cook *käsespätzle* almost as well as Father's late wife. She didn't fancy numbers as much as she did romantic literature, but wartime work was impossible to find, so she was content to—

Something fell from the sky.

A shadow blasted across the truck, briefly barricading the sun. An instant later, a machine of wood

3

and twanging wires flew across the truck's hood, missing it by the breadth of a hand. Smoke coiled out behind it. The howling contraption flipped in the air, bits of it snapping free even as it dropped, and then it struck a patch of wild forget-me-nots on the side of the road, crushed them, and vanished in the tall grass beyond.

Ellenor torqued the steering wheel to the right and applied brake and clutch, her breath trapped behind her teeth. The truck came to a jarring halt, the two white brood boxes sliding in the back and dislodging a hundred dead bees. Exhaling, she looked from the window in the direction of whatever the hell it was. The war rarely reached this far from the Front; she never fell asleep with the sound of German artillery pounding French hillsides, as so many others did. Other than the occasional supply convoy from the factories in Berlin, Father's estate and the villages nearby saw no evidence of the blood being hemorrhaged by millions a few dozen miles away. But Ellenor knew, staring from the truck's dusty window, a part of the war had almost crushed her. Its smoke rose like a serpent from where it waited in the grass.

She opened the door.

The truck was a 28-horsepower Daimler that Father had purchased five years ago, before the war had bent all civilian industry toward the military effort against France and—as the newspapers called them—the Damn Brits. Ellenor Jantz was one of the few women who could operate an automobile. In fact, she'd heard of only one other woman who drove, a stage actress in Stuttgart who was known to advocate for the right to vote, so it was a wonder she'd not yet been run out of town. Ellenor had been born in the New Mexico Territory to an American cattle rancher who'd taught his daughter many things, like how to drive and how to properly groom a horse. And also how to fire a gun.

She took the rifle from the truck as the smoke rose on gray wings from just beyond the pale blue forget-me-nots. Because she'd been inspecting the hives on the hill, she was dressed oddly: canvas trousers tucked into boots a size too large for her, a white top, and a veil-covered pith helmet hanging down her back, its chinstrap tight at her throat. She'd already removed her bulky goatskin gloves. She walked in the direction of the wreckage.

A plane lay crumpled in the German soil. Its wooden fuselage was cracked and bent inward, splinters everywhere. The propeller was little more than a stub, a deep gouge beneath it from where it had screwed itself into the ground. Wires sprang from boards, their ends split and quivering. Fuel burned in small patches in the weeds.

Two hours ago, when finding her bees either dead or absconded, Ellenor had said two words, which she repeated here now as she stood before the ruin that smelled of oil and melting wax: "What happened?"

The plane did not bear the Iron Cross insignia of Germany. Nor did she find any markings of the French enemy. Ellenor's green eyes scanned the mangled wood until she realized—

"It's British."

The blue, white, and red cockade flashed on the remaining tail section as boldly as a target, a defiant ring of color amidst the smoke. Ellenor lifted the rifle, a Mannlicher bolt-action she'd borrowed from Father's cabinet, the butt smooth against her shoulder. She'd attended a sideshow years ago and witnessed a woman named Annie Oakley shoot tossed coins from the sky, and Miss Oakley's reputation had nothing to fear from Ellenor Jantz. Still, Ellenor could surprise you at many things. She held the rifle steady as she circled what was left of the plane.

A man lay face down in the dirt.

He wore flyer's gear: a thick coat to ward off the cold, a leather skullcap, and a silk scarf too flamboyant ever to be permitted for use by the infantry; the scarf was the color of cobalt, an airman's affectation. One end of it was on fire.

Ellenor leaped forward and crushed her boot against the little flame, obliterating it. She knelt, putting her rifle on the ground, its trigger inches from her knee.

"Hello?"

He made no sound. Ellenor cursed silently to herself. She was terrified of the war and spent most days waiting for the boy from the next village to come with the latest news from the telegraph office. The radio in Father's study worked only intermittently; French bombs had unraveled too much infrastructure. And yet now the war had suddenly come to her, crashing into the hillside acreage of Father's estate and ejecting its pilot either dead or injured at her feet.

She put her hands on him, wishing she were still wearing her beekeeping gloves. The leather of his coat was cold but supple, obviously worn on many campaigns. "Can you hear me?"

She rolled him over.

He wore goggles with one smashed-in lens. His cheeks were smooth and bronze and slick with blood from his chin to his left ear. He smelled of gunpowder. The machine gun that had been mounted to his plane was bent and useless a few feet away.

Ellenor checked for a pulse. Is this how the physicians did it? A finger at the throat? She felt something, a steady rhythm—or was it her imagination? "Sir, can you hear me?" She carefully lifted his goggles—

He moved. Muscles firing, eyes flashing open, he shouted and lurched for her, hands grasping. She pulled back just in time, finding the rifle precisely where she intended it to be, pointing it at him even as she sprang to her feet.

He was feral. Feral and wounded and lost on the wrong side of the Front. Instinctively he reacted to save himself, snarling as he lunged straight at her with startling velocity.

Ellenor had never shot anyone before. Indeed, she'd never fired a weapon at anything other than the coyotes that used to torment her mother's hens. She'd brought the twenty-year-old Mannlicher from Father's study because he insisted she not go into the wilderness unarmed during times of war, even though the trenches were miles away. She told him it was unnecessary, but he was a man who insisted things and then *meant* those things, so she'd dutifully loaded the weapon and stowed it in the truck.

The pilot closed the small gap between them. Ellenor reflexively jerked the trigger. The eight-millimeter bullet blasted from the barrel.

He caught it.

The man whipped his hand in front of his face at the exact moment she fired. He snapped his fist around the incoming slug in midair, and it bored a hole through his palm and out the back of his hand. But he managed to alter its trajectory just enough that the bullet whispered an inch from his head, sparing his life.

Ellenor gasped. The airman fell, moaning, clutching his new wound to his chest.

She took several steps backward, working the rifle's bolt to chamber another round, stunned by what she'd nearly done. "Stop it!" she yelled at him, the rifle bobbing up and down in her panicked grip. She'd almost killed him, *would* have killed him had he not gotten lucky. She felt suddenly like vomiting into the grass. "Stay there or I'll kill you."

He must have believed her. More likely, he was startled to hear her speaking English. Either way, he rolled onto his side and then held still, injured hand pinched in his armpit, squinting up at her.

She fought to regain her breath. She'd come half a second from being a murderer. And the damn hat's chinstrap was choking her to death, but she couldn't risk taking a hand from the rifle. "I said not to move."

He coughed. "Does it bloody well look like I'm moving?"

"*Shut up.*"

He said nothing else. He laid his head on the ground, wincing, apparently becoming aware of all his injuries at once. He'd survived the crash by chance alone, but his body had paid for his good fortune. His bright blue scarf looked absurd against the blood and the dirt.

Ellenor's body finally relaxed. The tension still forced her cheek against the rifle's stock, but her heart came back down to earth. In a matter of minutes, she'd gone from lamenting two dead beehives to almost killing a foreign soldier. The day had begun in such an ordinary way, with mathematics lessons followed by English-language practice followed by a war report from the boy on the bicycle. Father had paid him with a pair of red apples and sent him on his way.

And now this. When she was certain the man wasn't about to launch another assault, she slowly began to move toward the truck, never letting the barrel's iron sights leave her target. The idea of trying to tie him up and haul him to the authorities was outlandish, so she'd report the matter to Father and let him—

"Don't leave me here," the pilot said.

She stopped. Yes, he was British. His accent said as much. And Ellenor, being American, should have been sympathetic—the two of them bound by the King's English and all—but her home country had only recently decided to wade uncertainly into the war, and so she felt no particular fealty to one side or the other. All wars were run by idiotic men in hats; they scrapped over land and religion and sent boys half their age to die in tangles of barbed wire or gas-filled holes. They were all the same.

"Please."

She lifted her cheek from the rifle's smooth wood. The British pilot looked up at her, blood ringing one blue-gray eye. He was doomed. The Front was too far. Whatever aerodrome served as his base somewhere in the French countryside might as well have been in outer space. He would not make it out of Germany, not torn half to bits like this. The *Polizei* would arrest him or the army would imprison him. Or perhaps he'd bleed to death here among the undeserving forget-me-nots. Flyers died violent deaths, their airplanes too ridiculous to remain for long in the sky.

He said something too softly for her to hear.

She looked down the dirt track that lay like a ribbon on the hillside. Father's house was still another mile, at least. A hundred yards from where she stood with her rifle, a deer nibbled on clover, unaware of the war, unaware of Ellenor and the decision she had to make.

She turned her attention back to the man she'd almost killed. "What did you say?"

He closed his eyes. "I have to…to find her."

"Find whom?"

He didn't say. The pain clubbed him, bound him, and dragged him down to darkness.

She lowered the rifle and sighed. She glanced back toward the deer, perhaps for moral support, but the animal had fled without sound.

Chapter Two

She used a rope and pulley to drag him into the truck.

The simple block-and-tackle rig was something Father had suggested for helping Ellenor manhandle the heavy hives. Each box, when filled with ten frames of honey to be harvested, could weigh as much as eighty pounds. Ellenor depended on physics to assist her, and eventually she winched the foreigner into position just behind the vehicle's cab. He slept and bled.

She unwound the blue scarf from his neck, intending to wrap the hand she'd shot, but the hole was nasty; it leaked slowly, continuously. Pressure would help, but the man was unconscious and not able to assist in his own first aid.

"Why bother?" Ellenor asked herself. Normally she'd talk with the bees, a delightful chorus of eager girls who reaped nectar and pollen from German wildflowers and ferried them into their homes. But she had no bees other than the dead, their corpses awaiting closer inspection in Father's barn. Instead, she talked to herself.

"Damned if I know."

The bleeding had to be stopped. Ellenor took the nearest hive box and removed the frames, wax-filled forms on which the bees constructed their hexagonal treasure boxes. Using a flat-bladed tool, she scraped the edges of the frames, building up a sticky wad of propolis, which was the beekeeper's term for processed tree sap. Bees used it for mortar and sealant. Ellenor could think of nothing more appropriate for her task.

She smeared the gummy residue across the pilot's palm, filling the jagged hole. She repeated this on the back of his hand, seeing in her mind how quickly his reflexes had reacted when she'd pulled the trigger. Had he been one microsecond slower, she would have shot him in the face.

She forced the thought away. Satisfied that her impromptu patch would suffice, she bound the long scarf around his hand and tied it off between his fingers.

The truck, as was often the case, failed to fire. Ellenor bit her lower lip and roughly repeated the routine until the engine coughed out whatever had been choking it and rumbled to uncertain life. Horses remained far more trustworthy. Most horses, however, had been requisitioned by the German government, along with the majority of the country's young men, able-bodied or otherwise. After several moments of uncertain shifting, Ellenor got the vehicle trundling down the hill. She left behind the still-smoking pile of wood and wire that had once been a British plane.

****

War had brought shovels to the Rhineland. Shovels, really, seemed to be more important than guns. Ellenor Jantz had watched crates of them being unloaded from trains, bundles of them cinched together with household twine, crude versions of them hammered into form at the blacksmith's forge. Countless variations of shovels had been taken west on trucks and motorbikes and hay wagons. The object of this obsession, it seemed, was the trench. Men dug trenches like animals, like demons, like madmen. You dug faster than the French or you died.

Father's estate was situated just far enough from this furious digging to avoid being enveloped by the chaos but close enough that you could bear witness to the constant back-and-forth if you stood on the library balcony and trained the telescope to the west. Father often lingered there with his schnapps, bent over the eyepiece, thinking his thoughts. Ellenor, who once adored the telescope and the heavens it revealed to her, now wanted nothing to do with it.

She guided the truck to the back of the stone barn, its masonry from a previous generation, its grand loft like something from a child's tale. Since hostilities had commenced three years ago, Father had dismissed many of his household staff, but the old Jewish stable-master, Josef, remained steadfastly at his post. He groomed livestock for a living but fancied himself an American cowboy. If fate had been kinder, Josef would have been employed in Buffalo Bill's Wild West Show.

Ellenor wasted no time. "Joe?" She hurried into the barn through one of its many well-oiled wooden doors, shifting automatically into German: "Josef, are you here?"

"Yes, Little Fox. Aren't I always?" He emerged from the tack room, tall and gnarled, his round-rimmed glasses too small for his face. "How's it look for this year's honey harvest?"

"I need your help."

"Since when does the American Joan of Arc need anyone's assistance?"

"A man was shot down in front of me."

He removed his spectacles, slowly, giving himself time to process what she'd said. "What do you mean *shot down*?"

"A flyer. He nearly crashed into the truck."

"I saw the smoke in the sky but…you're all right?"

"Josef, please. I brought him here."

"You—you *what*?"

She offered no further details. The longer the man lay out there in the open, the greater the chance he'd be discovered. Ellenor might have been brave on certain days, but she had no desire to be accused of harboring an enemy agent. "I need to get him inside, and I can't do it alone." She left the barn without waiting to see if Josef followed.

The airman was still asleep, his face drained of color. By the time she got him untangled from the pulley's rope, Josef was at her side, his agile hands making short work of the rope. Without further question, he gathered the pilot in his arms and carried him into the warm shadows of the barn. Ellenor had known Josef for only a year, but she trusted him as much as she'd ever trusted anyone. On her very first day at work here twelve months ago, he'd doffed his cowboy hat and said, "Howdy, ma'am," just like a rancher in a dime-store novel. Since then, she supplied him with honey biscuits and he told her Teutonic fairy tales he'd learned as a boy.

Josef settled the pilot to the floor in one of the empty stalls, then brought in a lantern for a closer look. "He fell from the sky, you say?"

"Right in front of me."

"Those damn flying contrivances are deathtraps.

14

Who is he?"

"He didn't say."

"You spoke to him?"

"Briefly. I believe he's from England."

"Of course he is. Cheeky bastards are hard to kill." Josef studied the man's injuries. "What about our boy?"

"Our boy?"

"The fellow from our side who sent this one here to the ground. Did you see a friendly plane circling overhead?"

"I didn't really think to look."

Josef used a rag from the pocket of his thick britches to dab the blood from the man's mouth. "I suppose it could have been engine failure. Or the propeller could have snapped off. Or a wing could have disintegrated. A man strapping himself into a wooden bird with a motor attached deserves whatever he gets." He looked up at Ellenor from where he squatted in the straw. "What do you intend to do with him? Tell Father that a puppy followed you home and beg to keep him?"

Ellenor had asked herself the same question on the drive down the hill. She felt like crying over her lost hives. She felt like being sick with the thought of almost becoming a murderer. She felt, most of all, like an outsider. She'd been born in the New Mexico Territory, which wasn't even a proper state of the Union until five years ago, and she'd spent the last year across the ocean in a country that had charmed her at first but now devoured its neighbors in never-ending war.

"Little Fox?"

"Will he live?"

Josef looked down at the man and shrugged one

substantial shoulder. "There is a Yiddish word: *bashert*. It is difficult to define in German, but *bashert* is what's meant to be. There are no coincidences in the universe. If this fallen angel of yours dies, it is *bashert*."

"And if he doesn't die?"

"Same thing." Josef pointed. "Now pull up that milking stool. You're going to play like a nurse for a while and see if you can help *bashert* decide one way or the other."

Chapter Three

Twenty-three hours before he crashed behind enemy lines, Alec Corbin-Dawes told the first lie of his adult life. "This corned beef pie is just as good as my mum makes back in Derby."

The Frenchman nodded, pleased. He'd been rich in his former life, before the war had forced him to share his chateau with a squadron of flyers who cared little for the sanctity of marble floors and the importance of the Degas hanging in the foyer. Though much of the man's wealth had been leveraged for the good of his country, his name still resonated with power, and now Alec needed some of that power if he were to embark on his unsanctioned mission. Hence the lie.

Nineteen hours before his petrol line was severed at five thousand feet, Alec carried the signed approval letter the Frenchman had given him and showed it to the guards at the munitions depot, gaining unfettered access to the weapons within. His plane was a barely adequate Avro 504, a two-seater used for training these neophytes who seemed far too willing to lift into the sky and die. Alec had been posted here across the Channel and far from home to teach them how to manhandle an aircraft that was likely to become their coffin. As a training platform, the Avro was not equipped with a gun.

Fourteen hours before he fell, Alec finished

mounting the Lewis machine gun on his crate, the Avro now casting a more sinister shadow on the ground. He loaded it completely, stuffing it with bullets, though hitting a flying target while careening through the air at ninety miles an hour was more luck than anything else. You were statistically more likely to shoot your own propeller off.

Ten hours before he watched the ground rush up at him, he joined the Frenchies in their canteen, smiling gently as they sang "La Madelon" and tried to drink enough to forget the math: the average lifespan of a flyer on either side of the Front was thirty days. Alec had been brought here to teach them because he'd managed to survive for over a year. They'd made him a lieutenant and counted his kills on a board behind the bar.

Three hours before he closed his eyes upon impact, he awoke from scant sleep and slipped from his billet even before the first dawn patrol had departed. No one flew at night because there was no point; you simply couldn't see. Alec pulled the chocks from the Avro's wheels and paid a half-drunk enlisted man five *francs* to spin the prop when he fired her up. Without permission, without second thoughts, he wrapped a blue scarf around his neck and rattled the plane along the dirt track until one pull of the stick tugged him up toward a sky full of sparkling stars.

One hour before he lay in the German dirt, too fractured to move, he remembered what his sister had said on the day she'd left England: "If you ever tire of drowsy Derby, little brother, come find me."

"You're only one minute older than I am," he'd reminded her.

"One is enough."

"Stay," he'd said.

"Come find me."

Three minutes before he opened his one working eye to see a rifle in his face, an Albatros D.V whispered into position behind him. Alec enjoyed an uncanny symbiosis with airplanes, and had he not been stuck in the ungainly Avro, he could have shrugged off his pursuer and probably turned him into prey. As it was, the single-seat Albatros devoured him, its dual Spandau guns shredding the back half of his plane.

The last thing he saw was a woman with green eyes.

Chapter Four

Josef shot a wild hog with a rifle he claimed was once owned by Billy the Kid.

"I don't believe you," Ellenor told him after checking on the pilot who slept in the stall.

"You shouldn't. I am a daydreamer."

Josef field-dressed the hairy animal. Ellenor conducted an autopsy.

The bees had died. The cause of death, however, remained unknown. The *Apis Mellifera* was the world's most interesting creature, at least in her opinion, but so much of it remained a mystery. How did bees build with such precision, each hexagonal cell tilted at precisely thirteen degrees? How did they know to cap those cells when the honey inside reached less than eighteen percent water content? How did they measure such things?

"With very tiny tools," she said to herself as she bent over the table. Using a magnifying glass, she studied the dead. The possible culprits were manifold: disease, poor nutrition, accidental poisoning, predators. Or, equally likely, the queen had failed her colony, and the bees had been unable to produce another queen to replace her.

At the far end of the vast barn, Josef hummed to himself as he butchered what would become the household's evening meal.

Ellenor looked for signs of abnormal wing shapes but wasn't able to concentrate on the task at hand. She couldn't stop thinking about the pilot. What had he said before passing out? *I have to find her.* That was not the kind of statement you expected from a man torn from the middle of a war. He might have said, *Where am I?* Or even, *I need to return to my squadron.* Those things made sense. Perhaps he'd been delirious from the pain.

She saw no misshapen wings. She'd already discounted the dreadful ailment known as chalkbrood, which transformed bees into white mummies. Chalkbrood was a fungal disease with very visible signs, none of which she observed here. So what was the next most likely cause?

The hog went straight from the barn to the kitchen. The brass bell at the back door would soon sound to call the staff to dinner.

She opened the stall door.

The flyer's face, now cleaned, had relaxed in his sleep. His hair was blond, his cheeks smooth. He looked like the captain of one of those rowing teams she had seen in Boston before she boarded the ship for Europe. A horse blanket covered him. His injured hand lay atop the blanket. Josef had removed the scarf, commended Ellenor on her use of the bees' propolis to stem the bleeding, and bound the wound in fresh linen. The Briton slept in peace.

She knelt beside him. *I have to find her.* She now had two riddles to solve: what killer had destroyed her bees, and what woman was the object of this man's quest?

By the time the bell clanged, she had washed herself of bee residue and British blood, and she spent the next hour with her adopted clan, everyone gathered at Father's enormous table made from a single slab of Black Forest oak. The yellow beeswax candles that Ellenor had made provided ample light, standing in ceramic dishes painted with scenes of the hunt. Everyone seemed in fine spirits, considering the circumstances. As was their custom, servants and family members dined together, enjoying human conversation as much as possible in the ugly shadow of war. The children, Karl and Truda, seemed immune to what was transpiring at the Front, sheltered by their dad and rendered immortal by their youth. They showed off their budding English skills and occasionally kicked each other under the table.

And then Father stood up.

Everyone quieted. Ellenor saw a change in the man who had hired her one year ago. Still robust, he'd relinquished a bit of his boyish candor. These days he kept many things to himself that he would have shared openly not so long ago. As patriarch, he saw his foremost duty to protect those within these walls, and that meant absorbing the full truth of what the Kaiser was doing with this endless war. Father had seen the torn-apart bodies being brought back from the so-called Hindenburg Line, the series of bulwarks the Germans had constructed to defend those parts of France they'd annexed. He'd seen the yellowed corpses of men who had choked to death on gas.

"Please, if you may," he said, and made a motion for them all to stand.

Chairs rasped against the tiles as everyone complied. They lined up in front of him like school kids on the first day of lessons. On Ellenor's right was the house's longtime cook, Dagmar. On her left was Roswalt, the butler. Father stood before them, wearing his second-best suit, a slip of paper in his hands. He seemed to be gathering his thoughts. The silence grew.

Ellenor, an optimist by nature, suddenly expected the worst.

Finally Father cleared his throat. Ellenor always enjoyed hearing him speak. He used the German language in the style of his generation, with crisp enunciation and nary a slang word to be found. "This morning I received a wire from the office of the *Luftstreitkräfte.*"

Ellenor knew it wasn't good news. If the German air force had contacted Father, it meant only one thing. She waited for him to say it.

"Due to the relative proximity of my acreage to the Front, and given the scope of my property and the diversity of its resources, it seems we're all being…conscripted into the war effort." He held himself composed, mostly majestic, allowing only the tiniest bit of emotion to show in his gray eyes. "The German High Command has seen fit to present us with a *Jagdstaffeln*, or hunting squadron, as they like to call it. The members of that squadron, under the command of Captain Gustov Voss, will make their residence here, in this very house, as early as tomorrow." Father looked at each of them in turn, starting with his children and sweeping the room, ending with Ellenor. "We are to provide them with every courtesy for the duration of their stay, however long it might be. Am I understood?"

They all spoke at once in the affirmative, family and staff ardently agreeing. He was, after all, Father. They would have agreed to swimming naked in the

Rhine had he asked.

"I apologize for the disruption this is sure to cause in our daily lives," he told them. "But our boys are being slaughtered not far from here and dying on barbed wire. I'm sure the least we can do is abide with the slight inconvenience of hosting the military for a while."

Several nods confirmed this. Any citizen of Germany should be honored to do their small part, and if that meant giving up their bedroom to a weary soldier, so be it.

Father must have seen something in Ellenor's face. He stared at her. "Miss Jantz?"

His sudden attention startled her. "Sir?"

"Are you troubled by this idea?"

"No, I…" She groped for some way to deflect him. "I'm just tired of all the fighting, I suppose."

"As am I. Is there something you'd like to say?"

"No, sir," she replied with her most reassuring smile, thinking about the British airman she'd hidden in the barn.

****

Just like one of his beloved biplanes rising from the fog, Alec Corbin-Dawes came back to life. His eyelids fluttered. His first thought upon waking was not of the pain nor of his sister nor of the crash. He thought instead about The Dragon.

The Scout Experimental 5 was the finest thing ever made in Hampshire, specifically in the thousand-year-old town of Farnborough. As an aircraft, the S.E.5 was nimble and deceptive, a wicked little crate with a V8 engine and a top end of one hundred and fifty miles an hour. Compared to the Avro he'd borrowed and subsequently crashed, the S.E.5 was a bolt of lightning from the clouds. Alec had flown one with St. George's dragon painted under the wing. He'd killed enough Huns in The Dragon that the papers back home had called him an ace.

His talent had kept him alive, and his longevity had earned him a reward in the form of a training assignment at a French aerodrome a few miles from the zigzag trenches of the Front. No longer did he lead patrols. No longer did he ride The Dragon like some goggle-wearing sorcerer, tormenting the German skies.

He opened his eyes fully, inhaling the scents of straw and horse and old wood.

Everything hurt like hell.

His ribs were bad, but not as bad as his left knee, which in turn had nothing on his hand, which had been fine—more or less—until the woman with the American accent had shot him. *Shot him.* His hand throbbed, the pain webbing outward from his palm to excite the tips of his fingers. A headache raged at both temples. And he'd almost bitten through his goddamn tongue.

Feeling perverse, he tried to sit up.

He slumped back immediately. The pain bubbled fast and then settled, holding at a low boil. If the woman had hauled him here to wait for the local police to come, he had no desire to wait around until—

The stall door swung open.

She'd changed clothes. Her odd ensemble of before had been replaced by an ankle-length skirt and sensible top, her sleeves buttoned at the wrists. She'd brushed her hair, the brown locks burnished with red in the light that spilled in from behind her. Her firearm was nowhere in sight.

"You're awake," she said.

Was it a question or an observation? Alec wasn't certain. But she was alone, without anyone nearby who had come to abduct him.

She kept one hand on the stall door, as if she might leap back out and slam it shut at any moment. "Can you hear me?"

He swallowed. "Aye."

She nodded, exhaling the breath she'd apparently been holding. "Who are you?"

Slowly Alec came back to himself, his wits returning, his resolve pushing through the pain. "Where am I?"

"In Bruni's milking stall."

"Bruni?"

"One of the cows. It was the best I had."

He used his good hand to touch the laceration on his head. He felt a bandage there.

"Got you stitched up, more or less. It was the least I could do, considering that I came very close to…well, at any rate, my name is Ellenor Jantz, instructor of English, mathematics, and civics, as well as a hobbyist beekeeper, and I need you to leave immediately because a squadron of German air officers is taking up residence here in the morning, at which point they'll arrest the both of us."

Alec absorbed this, sorting through the information she'd imparted. He raised an eyebrow, the only thing on him that didn't hurt. "A hobbyist *what*?"

The woman named Ellenor scowled. "Do you drink whiskey?"

"I've never turned it down. Irish?"

"Does it matter?"

"Not one damn bit."

"Good. I'll trade you a glass for your name."

That seemed fair enough. He'd given far more for a good swallow in his time. He told her his name and then added, almost as an afterthought, "Lieutenant, Royal Flying Corps."

And certified ace, the vain part of him wanted to say, but he had the notion that she wouldn't be impressed.

"I'll be back in a moment," she said, shutting the stall door behind her. He heard the wooden block fall into place, latching him inside.

Alec closed his eyes again. He'd been a stupid bastard to think he could locate his sister and bring her back to France without any difficulties along the way. He'd barely made it into Germany before falling victim to the rookie mistake of letting Fritz put him between the sun and a machine gun. He blamed his error on too much time training fresh-faced fools and not enough time keeping his edge in the air. How would he reach his sister now? How would he save her?

The woman named Ellenor Jantz returned, brown bottle in hand. "Do you understand what I've told you?"

"I believe so."

"That's not good enough. You cannot be here in the morning."

He wondered if he could sit up. Perhaps in a few minutes he'd try. "May I ask you another question?"

She seemed reluctant, but nodded.

"How far are we from the town of Metz?"

"Uh…at least a hundred miles, probably more. I'm

not sure. I've never been there."

So much for walking. He certainly couldn't travel that far on foot. Could he borrow an automobile? A horse? Bruni the milking cow? He didn't have much time...

Ellenor held out the bottle. "Who is she?"

Alec blinked, wondering if the American had somehow read his thoughts. Had he talked in his sleep?

"You told me that you had to find someone," she said. "Find *her*. Who is she?"

Alec remembered. Before losing his senses at the wreckage of the Avro, he'd blurted out the first and most important thing before succumbing to his wounds. Now, as he lay here, he knew it wasn't wise to reveal too much of himself, but maybe if this woman understood the danger, she'd agree to help him find a car. "*She* is Sarah, my twin sister. The French are going to bomb a factory at Metz in five days. Sarah works there. I have to get her out."

Chapter Five

"Darkness," Ellenor said, "is no time for bees."

"Are bees afraid of the dark?" Truda asked.

Ellenor smiled at the girl. "Bees fear nothing."

Karl looked unconvinced. "Everyone fears something."

Ellenor considered it. She sat in the children's room, surrounded by all the things a wealthy European bought for his children, which was everything. One wall was painted like an African savannah. Truda adored cleverly painted dolls that fit one inside the other. Karl's collection of wooden swords knew no equal on the Continent. "Bees don't come out at night," she explained. "Right now, as we sit here at our candlelight, all the bees are tucked safely in their hives. They've no business in the dark. They can't see the flowers, and they need the sun to guide them home." She showed them a biologist's illustration of a honey bee, its body parts meticulously labeled. "See these extra eyes? They're called *ocelli*. Those eyes allow the bee to navigate by the direction of the sun's rays."

"He looks weird," Karl said, frowning.

"It's a female."

"What?" Karl peered closer, perhaps expecting to see some kind of bee genitalia. "How can you tell?"

"The girl bees do all the work. The boy bees do nothing. Well, *almost* nothing." Ellenor decided this was no time to explain the mating habits of bees—or *any* mating habits, for that matter. "Here, look at this." She reached into the neckline of her top and removed a pendant on the end of a Swiss-made chain. The pewter ornament was in the shape of a bee, its body made of yellow feldspar. "Your father gave this to me after my first honey harvest last year. See how beautiful she is?"

"That's a girl?"

"It is. Suffice to say that a male bee has a boring and rather short life."

Truda found that funny, and Karl threatened to pinch her if she didn't stop giggling, and Truda dared him to try, and that was how it went while Ellenor glanced from the window at the starry sky and thought of Lieutenant Corbin-Dawes.

Leave it to a Brit to hyphenate a surname. How pretentious. Maybe he was the nephew of a duke or baron or someone else full of pomp and peerage. If he was half a gentleman at all, he'd vacate the barn to spare her the repercussions if the Germans discovered him here in the morning. Except, of course, he could barely move. He could hardly be expected to embark on a march back to the Front as if he were just a merry old chap with a whistle on his lips.

I have to find her.

He'd explained it like this: His sister, Sarah, had married an Alsatian industrialist who'd died of smallpox two years after the wedding. Sarah and her in-laws now operated the factory without him, supplying the Fatherland with engine parts for what the lieutenant called *lorries* but Ellenor knew as *trucks*. Corbin-Dawes had attended a strategic meeting at his aerodrome in which plans were revealed for a bombing flight on Sarah's factory. He'd taken a plane without permission in hopes of flying her back across a border she'd otherwise never be allowed to cross.

"Well, at least I'm not a boy bee!" Truda shouted at her brother.

Ellenor settled them down. Heaven forbid that Father should hear them all the way in his study, where he was probably bent over his journal, writing in his flowing penmanship about the impending guests. This time tomorrow he would likely relinquish that very room to Captain Gustov Voss, who would probably soil the carpet with his Prussian boots.

Maybe it was the thought of those boots that finally convinced her. It would be hard enough to bear the sight of interlopers mucking up the garden; Ellenor was not going to give them the pleasure of taking a prisoner.

She put Karl and Truda to bed at the usual hour, just as the children's clock, made in Bavaria, ferried out its little bird and clucked the time. Then it was off to bed herself, except not really, because while the house lay quiet under a blanket of summer stars, Ellenor slipped through the kitchen door and hurried barefoot to the man from England.

****

"Are you awake?"

Alec sat with his back against the slatted wooden wall. He'd managed to get himself at least partially upright. The bruises along his left side pulsed in pain, a ripple effect along the length of his body from where he'd slammed against the cockpit, the stick punching him in the ribs. The farrier, Josef, had fed him the remains of what must have been a fine meal. The mess hall back at the aerodrome knew nothing of food like this, rich and dark. "I'm here."

The door swung open, revealing the woman who'd both shot and saved him. She wore a long wool cloak and no shoes. Her hair was piled atop her head with a hasty array of pins. She wore no cosmetics. Alec was struck by her unadorned beauty.

"You look better," she said.

"German food is fortifying, even the leftovers."

"Josef fed you?"

"He seems a good fellow." *For a German*, he wanted to add. The Boche had burned a French village only three days ago. Alec saw no honor in razing the land as you conquered it. "What are you doing here?"

"I came to see if you're feeling well enough to move."

"No, I mean, here in Germany. You're American."

"I work here. Like your sister, I suppose."

"You came before the war?"

"No. I was touring the Continent. The previous teacher employed here got conscripted and sent to the Front, like most men of that age. Father advertised for someone who could speak English."

"Father?"

"He owns this very barn in which you hide."

"Ah. My thanks to him."

"He doesn't know you exist. He's a patriot. Now, before Father or anyone else learns of my deception, we need to get you out of here. The *Jagdstaffel* arriving in the morning will surely conceive of creative ways to deal with both of us if they find out."

Alec had been considering this. A *Jagdstaffel*, more commonly known as a *Jasta*, was a fighter squadron of elite pilots. They were given license to behave in ways completely alien to the infantry troops. They lived lavishly, painted their crates eccentric colors, and died by either burning alive or falling to their deaths. If they were being billeted here, it meant two things. One, the property was near enough to the Front to provide a choice launching point. Two, the facilities here could provide for the needs of men who were simultaneously violent, charming, haughty, and intense.

And there was something else, wasn't there? An opportunity waiting to be seized?

"What are you thinking?" Ellenor asked.

"Where will you have me go?"

"To the hives."

"I'm sorry?"

"Up on the hill. It's about two miles, if you follow the track. I have four beehives there...well, two, actually. But there's a shed where I keep my equipment, the supers and smoker—"

"Supers and smoker?"

"Never mind that. You can stay there. No one else is around. You'll be alone until you're well enough to travel. I'll bring food and other supplies tomorrow afternoon."

Alec looked at her anew. He already knew not to test her—his wounded hand was evidence of that—but he saw more in her eyes than a woman not afraid to defend herself. She risked her livelihood by helping him. She'd formulated a plan. She was definitely not the average lass one met on the train to London. "Do you speak German?" he asked,

"*Natürlich spreche ich Deutsch.*" She gave him an annoyed look. "Of course I speak German."

"My apologies. My wits are dulled. I'll get better, I promise. What I meant is, when these men are here, and you're among them on a day-to-day basis, if there's anything...*important* that is said among them, anything that might be useful..."

"If you're asking me to spy on our German house guests, then the answer is that I'm already planning on it."

For the first time in days, Alec smiled. It hurt his swollen lip. "Thank you."

"I'm not doing it for you, Mr. Corbin-Dawes of wherever the hell in England you're from. I'm doing it to try and keep my friends as much out of harm's way as possible."

"I meant thank you for making me smile."

"Oh." She seemed at a sudden loss. "Well...at any rate—"

"*At any rate*," he interrupted, "you tried to kill me, and now you're offering to protect me, and I'm accepting with as much grace as my tired body can muster. So, yes. I'll stay in this shed of yours, with the smokers and the soup."

"Supers. It's what we call the boxes for bees."

"Ah, beekeeper jargon. Perhaps one day I'll trade you for aeronautical jargon and we'll have a grand time discussing dope cans and Immelmann turns. In the meantime, I suppose I should attempt to get on my feet. But...you said this hiding spot is two miles away? I probably can't walk two yards, much less anywhere close to two miles, I'm afraid."

"You won't have to walk."

"How am I getting there?"

"I'm driving you—what do you think?"

"You know how to operate an automobile?"

She stared at him. "Don't make me shoot you again."

Alec surprised himself by smiling a second time. "Warning received."

When she helped him stand up, he managed not to scream.

Chapter Six

The next morning, Ellenor distracted herself from thoughts of the fugitive she'd concealed by writing a eulogy for the dead. In a journal bound between rugged hemp covers, she recorded every detail of her modest honey operation. Last year she'd harvested over a hundred pounds from three hives, and after splitting one of those colonies in two, she'd hoped for even more production this time around. But some damn thing had killed half her population.

She'd inherited the bees from one of Father's aging colleagues, a man he'd met as a young cavalry officer in the Franco-Prussian War, which he still referred to simply as "70/71." Having learned the art and science of apiculture on the farm back home in the States, Ellenor had jumped at the chance to add honey to the estate's list of home-grown products, along with grain, root vegetables, milk, butter, and eggs from the dozens of chickens that roamed freely and were occasionally poached by foxes at night. Father had brewed a batch of honey-flavored beer.

Ellenor kept her records in English because it was easier that way; she was fluent in German but had never been comfortable writing it. She kept track of everything: each inspection, every frame of capped and uncapped brood, all the activities that happened when the hive box was closed and only fully understood when it was opened. A healthy queen could lay two thousand eggs in a single day. She mated once and lived her entire life in the dark—except when Ellenor lifted the lid and peered inside. Comparing the notes she'd made yesterday on the hill with those she'd penned after inspecting the dead bees last night, she hoped to find some meaning behind the loss.

"Beautiful day, isn't it?" Dagmar called from the garden.

"Lovely."

"I'm terribly sorry about your bees."

"Thank you. We'll manage." *Will we?* Just because two colonies vanished didn't mean the other two were threatened. On the other hand, disease could certainly travel between hives.

"Any notion as to what happened?" Dagmar asked, basket in both hands.

"I'm still studying the problem. I'll let you know."

"Very good. See you for lunch, sweetie."

Ellenor smiled in what she hoped was an authentic way. Then she let the smile fall from her face and wrote *Investigation ongoing* in her field journal. Predators weren't to blame, as a family of hungry raccoons wouldn't have stopped until all four hives were disassembled and plundered of their riches. Besides, Ellenor had secured the top covers with wire, and raccoons might be agile little pests but they weren't capable of outwitting heavy-gauge wire—were they?

She felt the sound before she heard it. The air seemed to quiver slightly. Ellenor looked up from her work, aware that something had changed. She cast her eyes skyward and saw them.

A dozen black shapes appeared below the clouds.

The exhaust from their engines marred an otherwise blue sky. From here, the noise was little more than wasps buzzing, but with every passing second, it grew.

Josef emerged from the barn, neck craned back. Karl and Truda ran up, knees dirty, shielding their eyes from the sun. Doors opened in the main house. Faces appeared. Father stood on the library balcony.

The planes came.

The *Jasta* flew in an uneven formation, each biplane an individual miracle; how those radical, wooden things remained aloft was anyone's guess. The sound intensified. The men in those planes would now use Father's estate as a base from which to launch their sorties against the French. Since the war began three years ago, aviation had transformed the struggle. At first dismissed as a gimmick, the airplane had quickly become a scourge. And now the scourge was here.

They flew directly overhead with a howl, twelve dark crucifixes against the sky.

Without speaking, the family members and staff of the ancestral house in the Rhine valley watched the squadron turn, decelerate, and come closer to the ground. There was no particular grace to it; the biplanes shuddered, the pilots at their sticks little more than uniformed boys. And then, one by one, the aircraft touched down in the barley field two hundred yards behind the barn, their wheels kicking up plumes of soil.

Ellenor counted eleven single-seat units and one larger version built for two. They were painted according to the taste of the pilot, with daggers and hearts and wild jolts of color, personalized and cherished. The canvas was stretched taut across their wing decks, mended here and there from enemy fire.

Karl clapped and whooped as only a boy could do. His younger sister also seemed pleased, staring at the machines as if they were pages torn from a book and coming to life in front of her. Men had been flying for only a few years. Truda hoped that one day girls could fly, too.

Josef stepped up beside Ellenor. They watched the planes slow down in the field and form a line facing west, their motors eventually rattling to a stop. One by one the pilots climbed from the cockpits, stepped onto the lower of the wing decks, and leapt to the ground. Incredibly, one of them had a dog.

Josef said softly, "*A gast iz vi regen az er doi'ert tsu lang, vert er a last.*"

Ellenor kept her eyes on the man in the lead, a figure in a white coat. "I'm waiting."

"'A guest is like rain. When he lingers too long, he becomes a nuisance.'"

Father passed by, a happy child holding either hand, on their way to welcome the new arrivals.

"I suppose we'll see," Ellenor said.

Josef nodded. "Indeed."

****

Alec got up from his cot in a windowless shed that smelled of wax and stepped outside.

Even as he steadied himself in the morning sun, aware of every tiny joint in his body, he admitted the loveliness of this foreign landscape before him. The grasses sweeping down the hillside were deeper green than any he'd seen in Derbyshire. Towering beech trees, generations old, stood like thick sentinels, watching him without judgment. Even the track cut into the hill was lovely, a lazy brown lane leading down from his hiding place to the lustrous valley below.

War seemed so far away.

Yet if one mounted a swift motorbike and headed west, in a matter of hours the trees were broken in half by the constant shelling and no grass grew. The zone between the spirals of razor wire—No Man's Land— was a gray hell of body parts and holes. The men who lived in those rat tunnels were something Alec never wanted to be: the PBI, the Poor Bloody Infantry. They ate shitty stew and slept in mud up to their shins. When their commanding officers forced them to go over the top and charge enemy gun emplacements, half of them were chewed up by incoming fire. The lucky ones got hit by artillery and died instantly. The unluckiest got carried back as a basket case—a living torso and head without arms or legs.

Alec shivered. He was a flyer, and in comparison to the PBI, he lived the life of a god.

Yet even gods fell to earth.

And now, fallen, he had to find his wings. Last night he'd considered venturing to the nearest town and locating the telegraph office. He'd discarded this plan seconds later. Any word to Sarah would alert the Germans of the pending attack, as the telegraph operators at either end would reveal any message that sounded even slightly suspicious. Dozens of French flyers would be met with anti-aircraft fire—the dreaded *ack-ack*—and never return to their beds. Alec had to get his sister beyond the city of Metz and preferably out of Germany entirely without revealing the raid. And all of this had to happen in the next four days.

When the planes appeared overhead, Alec wasn't surprised. Miss Jantz had foretold their arrival. He watched them until they sank too low to be seen, their engines fading. They'd landed somewhere near the chateau where Miss Jantz worked as governess or tutor or whatever the devil she was. His left hand still felt on fire. At least she'd not delivered him to the Huns.

For lack of a proper plan, Alec started walking.

Two miles separated him from the house. On a normal day, on level ground, a man on foot could make two miles in only an hour, maybe even less. But Alec was battered; his knee complained with every step, and his spine was akin to an unoiled accordion. So he allotted himself two hours for this slow hike in the German countryside. At least he was moving downhill.

Mourning doves sounded their soft calls from the nearby trees as if nothing was wrong.

Alec's clothing would not reveal him for what he was. He'd left his uniform at the aerodrome in France, not wanting to risk his comrades if he were captured and interrogated. So as he made his way along the wheel-rutted path, he looked precisely like what he was: a man with a bandaged hand, limping slightly, bearing no ill will toward anyone.

He made it in less than two hours. Keeping to the tree line, he drew as near to the grounds as he dared. Had some observant onlooker seen him skulking about, he wouldn't have had an excuse for his actions. He looked like a spy. He crouched low in a thicket of wild blueberry bushes and looked upon the future of air conflict.

The newly introduced Fokker Dr.I had three decks of wings, a triplane capable of flying at least a hundred and eighty miles without refueling. The craft possessed equal parts range and agility. Even the propeller was beautiful, eight and a half feet of layered walnut and birch, polished to a deep shine. Mounted in front of the pilot's seat was a pair of 7.92-millimeter guns, synchronized to fire through the spinning prop. The plane was menacing and honorable and savage, like a waiting wolf.

And there were eleven of them.

"Son of a bitch." Alec had seen photographs. He'd read the briefs. But only now did he understand why supremacy in the sky was being won by Germany and the Central Powers. In April alone, the Allies had lost two hundred and fifty aircraft compared to the *Luftstreitkräfte*'s casualties of a mere sixty-six.

As much as Alec would have loved to fly one of those stunning crates, his mission necessitated the two-seat reconnaissance plane parked between the Fokkers—the Rumpler C.IV. The name was not romantic, but that was Fritz for you; the Germans made every word sound like a fist hitting meat. With a wingspan of over forty feet but an overall length of less than thirty, the bird looked dreadfully front-heavy, but Alec knew otherwise. He'd studied enough German planes to know that the Rumpler's water-cooled Mercedes engine could lift it to an elevation of over twenty thousand feet. It featured two machine guns, one facing forward and the other ring-mounted for the gunner in the back.

It also carried two hundred pounds of bombs.

Alec intended to steal it.

Chapter Seven

Men in hiding needed to eat. Ellenor packed an oilskin bag with rye bread and sausages, sauerkraut, and of course a jar of honey. Part of her said, *Let him starve up there.* Another part said, *He is not in need of saving.* And a third, more reckless part said, *Could be worse: at least he's not ugly.*

With a slight smirk, she filled a canteen with well water.

"Am I interrupting?"

She turned too quickly, sending the bread knife flying. It struck the kitchen floor and slid under the heavy butcher's block.

"I apologize for startling you, madam," Captain Voss said, hurrying in to retrieve the knife. "Please forgive my intrusion."

"There's nothing to forgive. Of course. It's fine."

"I'm an ogre."

"Not at all."

He held out the knife, handle first. "All the same, I'm sorry."

She assured him with a nod. Gustov Voss was not yet thirty years old but was known as the Grizzled by the men who served him, though he was smoothly shaven and without a single strand of gray in his close-cropped hair. He wore a light woolen sweater with the sleeves pushed to his elbows, revealing pronounced forearms and a wristwatch; Ellenor had read about the recent trend of wearing small clocks on bracelets, but other than a photograph in the newspaper, she'd never seen one in use.

"My name is Voss," he said. "Would you...like your knife back?"

"Oh. Yes. Thank you." She accepted the silly thing and felt a fool.

"Headed out for a picnic?"

"I'm sorry?"

He smiled. "Let me start over. This never happened. I never spooked you. You never lost your knife." He spun a complete circle on the heel of his black riding boots. "Hello, my name is Gustov Voss, fine kitchen you have here, and you are...?" He extended his hand.

Ellenor allowed a bit of the tension to leave her body. There was no peril here. "I am Ellenor Jantz. A pleasure to meet you, Mr. Voss."

They shook. "The pleasure is mine. Now then, I do hate to trespass, but I was wondering where a fellow could get his hands on a bottle of spirits."

"Alcohol?"

"Yes, it's a matter of preserving the supply, really, because if my men find it before I do, they'll deplete the inventory entirely. Believe me. I've seen them soak up the stain from a bar with a rag just to wring the last drip onto their tongues."

Ellenor permitted herself a partial smile. "Then for all our sakes, I should show you to the wine cellar."

"Does this wine cellar have a lock and key?"

"Yes."

"All the better. Lead on."

Nine limestone steps descended into the catacombs below the house, where the world smelled of roots and rain. Jars of preserved vegetables sat heavily on bent pine shelves that were no longer reliably capable of supporting the load. Another cave-like room held oaken barrels of ale—most of it brewed by Father—and a modest wine collection that had dwindled since 1914 when hostilities cut off the supply of all French vintages.

"These are Italian and Spanish wines, mostly," Ellenor explained as Voss tilted his head to examine the bottles with an oil lamp. "Corvina, Vermentino, an Amontillado—"

"Like the story?"

"Story?"

"By that writer Poe, the American."

The American. Ellenor's German was nearly flawless, and she only now realized that Captain Gustov Voss had no idea she wasn't a native-born *Fräulein* herself. "I'm not familiar with that story. He wrote the poem about the raven?"

Voss inspected the next shelf. "He did. I won't embarrass myself by reciting it to you."

Ellenor watched him as he prowled the inventory. Even out of uniform, he looked like a military officer. He moved like one.

"Ah, the true treasures, at last." He'd located the crates of vodka. "I hear the Russian flyers are not particularly talented, but I do share their love of drink. May I?"

"It's not mine to give."

"I'll pay for it. You will not find us to be ungrateful boarders."

"I'm sure Father wouldn't accept any payment for his hospitality."

"Yes, he strikes me as one of the last of the true patriots." Voss hefted a bottle of the clear liquid. "And you?"

"You're asking if I'm a patriot, or if I drink vodka?"

A new thought seemed to occur to him. "Are you his daughter?"

"I'm his employee. I teach his children."

"And everyone calls him Father?"

"We do."

"I see. Then I will do the same." He smiled and motioned upstairs. "Shall we?"

Once back in the kitchen, Voss plied her with more questions, asking about the crops, the horseflesh, the frequency of news from Berlin. In a matter of minutes she learned much about him in return. His father had taught him chess but he hated it. His mother had taught him Mozart but he preferred American ragtime. He knew how to hunt and how to box but also how to mend his own socks. "Perhaps I was a tailor in a past life," he mused.

"A past life?"

"The Buddhists believe one is reincarnated upon death. Would you agree?"

"I was told that heaven waits, after we die."

"The tone of your voice tells me you have your doubts."

She crossed her arms. "Mr. Voss, have you questioned everyone in the house in this manner? Or have I been selected because I know the location of the wine cellar key?"

He held up a hand in apology. "Forgive me, madam. I've spent the last two weeks cloistered with the same dozen men, listening to the same conversations and playing in the same endless card games. Frankly, the jokes were getting a bit old. I'm quite happy to be here."

"We're happy to host you."

Voss bid her farewell and took his leave, tossing the vodka bottle from one hand to the other without apparent concern for dropping it. He whistled "The Entertainer" as he went.

Ellenor looked down and realized she was still holding the knife.

****

Alec removed his shirt and examined himself in the summer sun.

Upon hiking back up the hill to the shed, he'd slept without dreaming. When he woke, he felt better but didn't trust the feeling; only a physical inspection would finally convince him that he'd been driven to the ground by enemy fire and had managed to survive. There was talk among the leadership in the Royal Flying Corps that certain flyers should begin experimenting with the safety devices sometimes employed by dirigible operators—parachutes. But those billowing sheets with their ropes and strings were just as likely to strangle you as save your life.

"Hello there," he said to a nebula of bruises along his side. His ribs weren't cracked, and over the course of the last few hours, the pain had subsided to a governable level. Alec had always been fit, his torso tight with muscle, but that muscle had done him no favors. A fat man had more padding against a fall.

That made him grin. He needed more porridge and cream, to be sure.

He tested his arms by making big arcs in the air. His shoulders moved in their sockets without complaint. His left hand remained mostly unusable. How long would it take a hole like that to heal? He rolled his neck deliberately, enjoying the crackling sensation; it was the sound of still being alive.

The truck chugged up the hill.

Alec located his shirt. He'd rinsed it out in a ceramic basin after giving it a few passes with a cake of lye. He'd brought along a spare set of clothing from his footlocker at the aerodrome, along with a few other small items, but all of that was in his rucksack, which had likely burned in the crash.

He pulled on his shirt and buttoned it one-handed.

He intended to wait until nightfall, advance quietly down the hill, and attempt to reach the Rumpler unseen. He would seize the Germans' plane from them while they slept only a few yards away, then fly that fat bird to Metz, land outside the city, and locate Sarah before the French filled the sky with their Breguet bombers and lethal Spad fighter escorts. Together he and his sister would get back safely across the line. Sarah was as obstinate a woman as God had ever made, but she always listened to her twin brother when there was serious business about. She trusted him as she trusted no other. Had Jesus Christ appeared before them and asked her to stand beside Him, she would have first asked Alec if she should, just to make sure. She might protest when Alec explained what was happening, but she'd damn sure get in that stolen plane if the alternative was being caught in the flames. Nowhere in

Metz would be safe that night.

Miss Jantz's truck drew closer.

Alec faced only one problem with his plan: aircraft required two personnel to fire the engine, one to work the ignition process in the cockpit and the other to give the prop a spin. Usually that task fell to the officer's mechanic or personal valet, commonly known as his batman, named after the pack-saddles or *bats* of the old cavalry days. Working as a team, pilot and batman put the crate into the air.

He might be able to button his shirt with one hand, but he could not start that plane alone.

The truck stopped noisily, barking out one last snort before quieting. He watched Miss Jantz open her door and climb out, her hair in a single braid down her back, her beekeeper's trousers tucked into her boots. She fetched a pith helmet from the seat and slammed the door.

"Desperate times, old chap," he said to himself.

She approached him, stopped, stared, and then said, "You owe me, Mr. Corbin-Dawes."

It wasn't what he'd expected from her. He nodded twice. "True enough. I might have died if not for you. I'll give you a pardon for the gunshot wound if you promise to please stop calling me *mister*."

"What should I call you, then?"

"My mother named me Alec."

"I don't believe I know you well enough."

"I'm easy to get to know. Even Americans like me." He tried a smile; he had to keep her on his side if he were to convince her of what needed to be done. "Granted, I've met only a few Colonials in my time, but I've heard nothing but good things about New York."

"I've never been to New York. I'm from New Mexico. We're not very fond of easterners." She held out the helmet, around which was wrapped a light fabric veil. "Come on. You can help me find the queen."

Alec wasn't entirely sure what she meant by either *easterners* or *the queen*, but he fell into line half a pace behind her, obedient and curious and biding his time.

"I brought food," she said.

"I appreciate it."

"It's not much. How long are you planning on staying?"

"Ah. Well. There's the rub, as Shakespeare would say."

"Meaning what?" She glanced back at him. "Are your friends out looking for you?"

"Hardly. As it turns out, I'm rather alone."

"How will you make it back across the Front?"

He shrugged. His plan was outrageous. "I'll think of something."

She opened the shed where he'd slept and brought out a collection of tools. She arrayed these items on the ground. "The hives are just over that rise, between those pines. There are two colonies left. We're going to open the brood chambers and inspect the queen's progress."

"You're talking about the queen bee."

"Of course. I lost two colonies. I need to ensure that these two are still healthy. They're all I've got left, and I want to check inside, see what's going on, make sure the queen is laying properly. But the boxes can be quite heavy."

"So I'm you're hired muscle."

"Not hired. I don't pay."

"Excellent. I've a long history of working miserable hours for inadequate pay. I'm in the military, after all."

That almost made her smile, but not quite. "We'll need to light the smoker first. Do you have matches?"

"I'm afraid they burned up with my cigarettes and the rest of my kit, back at the crash. I had food there, spare clothing, and a Webley revolver my captain gave to me the day I left for France."

"When we're finished here, we can try to locate your lost things where you went down."

"Not much reason for that, I should think. I don't anticipate shooting my way out of Germany, and I suspect the fire claimed everything else. Besides, you've done enough for me already. At any rate, I've no matches."

Ellenor fetched flint and steel from a tin inside the shed. She put dried pine needles into a metal can with a cone-shaped lid, then got the needles burning. A few seconds later, a line of black smoke issued from the can. "Let's go."

Alec carried the tools. He watched her obliquely as they walked toward the pines, the sun casting warm shadows beside them. What was she doing out here? An American expatriate in rural and rustic *Deutschland* in the middle of a war—she was as puzzling as she was lovely. She stood four inches shorter than Alec himself, with a slender jaw and eyes the color of the grass on which she walked. She wore no jewelry. She needed none.

They passed between the pine trees, and on the far side of the hill, supported on short stone platforms, were two stacks of white boxes. Each stack stood three boxes high. They were awash in what looked to be a hundred million bees.

Alec stopped.

"Put on the veil," she said, and kept walking.

He fumbled the hat to his head, found it to be too small, removed it, adjusted the strap, then tried again, all the while watching her as she moved among the shifting cloud of buzzing wings. Fearlessly she knelt beside one of the stacks and scrutinized the narrow opening in the bottom box.

Alec buttoned his sleeves at the wrist, thrust his hands into his pockets for protection, and slowly approached.

Without looking up, she told him, "The foragers, all females, bring back nectar and pollen, and other bees help them remove the load so they can head back out again. They can find food and water up to two miles away."

Alec halted ten feet from her, holding still. "How, uh…how do they find their way back?"

"No one knows for certain. If you look closely, you can see the bundles of pollen on their rear legs. It's fascinating, really."

"I'll take your word for it."

"They won't hurt you unless you're aggressive." Wearing neither veil nor gloves, she watched them in silence for a solid minute, unperturbed when they alighted on her hair. Finally she stood, took the lid from the nearest box, and held her burning can over the fury inside, drenching the bees with smoke.

"What the bloody hell are you doing?"

"Calming them."

"It calms them to choke on smoke?"

"They're not choking."

Alec watched in wonder, his veil occasionally probed, his plan momentarily forgotten.

She set the can aside and lifted a wooden frame from the middle of the box. It was a slab of honeycomb with hundreds of bees clinging to either side. She held it close to her face and squinted.

"What are you looking for?"

"Eggs."

"And…do you see any?"

"The queen's laying, all right. I see brood in different stages, some of these less than three days old." She leaned the frame against the outside of the box and pulled on a pair of gloves that covered her to the elbows. "The smoke has most likely driven her into the bottom box. This is where you earn your keep."

"Right." He exhaled. "For king and country, and all that…" He headed into the chaos of wings and noise. As the bees surrounded him, he wanted to laugh at his own timid response. He'd performed barrel loops thousands of feet off the ground. He'd shot men dead in their cockpits, their planes silently turning like falling leaves all the way to the ground. Other times he'd raked them with so many bullets that their petrol caught fire and they burned alive during their descent. He'd lifted off and landed safely more often than ninety percent of all pilots in the RFC, and here he was, frightened of angry insects.

"Something funny?" she asked.

"Just delirious, darling." Instantly realizing what he'd said, he gave her an apologetic look. "Forgive me. That *darling* part just came out. I didn't mean to—"

"That's all right."

"It's just that being a pilot...I mean, in the military we get rather..."

"I said it's all right." She smiled gently at him to let him know. "Now can you please lift this damn box for me?"

He lifted the damn box.

A whirlwind waited within. The box was heavy, perhaps four and a half stone—over sixty pounds—but his aching body responded. His strength was returning. The load wasn't easy on his left hand, so he set the box down quickly, bees everywhere. They didn't seem particularly intent on attacking him, but rather more anxious than anything else. "Now what?"

"Now we look for what doesn't want to be seen." Placing the smoker aside, she used a small steel pry bar to work free one of the ten frames in the lowest box. She extracted it slowly, holding it by its edges with the sun over her shoulder; bees covered it entirely.

"An odd occupation, beekeeping," Alec observed.

"No odder than flying in the air."

"I'll grant you that. May I ask you a personal question?"

"You needn't request permission." She carefully removed a second frame. "Besides, I already know what you're going to ask, and the answer is *dandelions*."

He had no idea what to make of this. "I...suppose I was going to ask how you came to be here in Germany, speaking the language so fluently, raising bees..."

"I left my home and crossed the Atlantic because of a dandelion growing outside my bedroom window. I'd just finished reading *The Prisoner of Zenda*. Are

54

you familiar with the book? At any rate, I was feeling adventuresome. I wanted action and derring-do. I was also younger and much more prone to girlish fancies. I went straight outside, plucked the dandelion from the ground, blew its little pieces into the wind, and made a wish."

"You wished for adventure?"

"Essentially, yes. I wanted to be Somewhere New." She said those two words with clear capitalization. "I hadn't the faintest idea where I might find Somewhere New, but that very evening I met the new owner of a Bavarian bakery, and two days later I was learning German from his wife."

"Your wish came true?"

By now she'd made it to the fifth frame in the box, her face less than a foot away, fearless without her veil, her eyes searching the crawling, humming mass. "I manage to put money away every month," she said. "Father pays me adequately, and I couldn't ask more from my surroundings. It's a lovely life."

"You mastered the language quickly."

"Perhaps I've been here longer than you think."

"I suppose that could be true. For some reason I assumed that you were—"

"Found her!" She got to her feet and motioned him closer with a tilt of her head. "Come see."

Alec did as she instructed. He gazed at the frame with its countless little cells, some of them capped with a hard brown shell, many of them open and holding little bits of color. He followed where she pointed until his eyes located a bee twice as long as the others, escorted by a retinue of agitated attendants. "That's the queen?"

"She looks healthy."

"I...suppose she does."

"Do you see how the cells around her hold little grains of rice? Those are eggs. And she's managed to find just about every cell without missing any, which is very good news. There's nothing worse than a spotty brood pattern."

He nodded gravely under his helmet. "I do so hate a spotty brood pattern."

Then something amazing happened: Miss Ellenor Jantz laughed. She shook her head at him, smiling, and then returned the queen's frame to the brood box, along with the others. A few minutes later, they'd packed everything back up as they had found it, leaving the bees to recover from the intrusion. As they returned to the shed, Alec removed his headgear. "You answered my first question in a way that was both surprising and satisfactory. May I ask you another?"

She hesitated before replying. "Why do I get the feeling this is one I may not want to hear?"

"Because you're intuitive. I'm going to ask you to—"

She held up a hand and stopped him. "Let's just enjoy the walk for a while before you go and spoil it."

He saw the wisdom in that. "Agreed."

And so he found himself talking to this woman about normal things, things that they could see and hear and touch, things they found important or frivolous, things that revealed quiet pieces of themselves, and just before he changed his mind, Alec asked her to be his accomplice.

Chapter Eight

Ellenor said no.

"Please, if you'll just hear me out…"

"There's nothing to hear. I won't be party to…to whatever you're proposing."

"You'd rather me wait out the war's end here in your tool shed?"

"Of course not."

"Then at least consider it. Please."

She saw the desperation in his blue eyes and was not moved by it. He could be charming one moment and distant as the horizon the next, and now he was somewhere in the middle, simultaneously manipulative and honest. Had they met before the war, say in a train station on a shared bench, what would they have discussed? Books? Art? The rising popularity of the telephone?

"Tell me what you're thinking," he said.

After a moment, she sighed. "If I were to aid you, I'd betray Father and all my friends."

"You're not betraying anyone. I'm not some kind of saboteur out to cripple the German war effort. I'm not planning on hurting anyone or stealing secret documents or—"

"You're stealing an entire airplane."

"Yes, quite. You're right. I'm taking something that doesn't belong to me. I'd pay for the bloody thing if I could, or have it shipped back when I'm done with it, but neither of those actions seems very practical at the moment. I just want to save my sister."

"I understand that."

"If you understood it, you'd see that I have no choice in the matter. I lost a dogfight and got shot down. By the grace of the old gods, I survived. And I *will* save my sister, who likes to remind me that she's one minute older than I am. I want to hear her say that again. And after I get her the hell out of Germany, I'll return to my aerodrome and face a military court-martial, and even if they throw me in a French jail until the war is over, it will be worth it. Sarah will be safe."

"There's no way to contact her?"

"What would you suggest? A letter? The post hasn't traveled between countries here in three years. Same can be said for the telegraph service. Perhaps I'll tie a string to a pigeon's leg."

She raised an eyebrow. "Sarcasm isn't becoming."

"Oh, there's nothing sarcastic about it, Miss Jantz. Believe me, I've considered all options, no matter how farfetched they might sound."

"And after all of that consideration, you've concluded that I'm the only thing standing in the way of your reunion with your sister."

"What's standing in my way are miles and miles of German wilderness. I need that plane. But I can't get it without your assistance. It is physically impossible."

"And after you fly away, then what happens to me?"

"What do you mean?"

"They'll know I helped you."

"You'll tell them that I forced you to cooperate."

"You forced me?"

"At gunpoint or something. I made you do it. They'll have no reason to believe otherwise."

"So I'm to play the role of the terrified damsel in this game of yours?"

"It's no game."

"Isn't it? You flyers are all the same, aren't you? You behave like boys without rules, rich little vandals who do whatever they please. I read the newspapers, Mr. Corbin-Dawes. I know the stories of pilots wearing tuxedos in their planes because they'd been carousing in Paris or Munich until sunrise, drinking and fornicating. I've heard about the license you're given by your senior officers to do as you please so long as you all keep killing the enemy in between the clouds."

"Most of those pilots you're reading about will die before their mid-twenties."

"And that's your excuse for recklessness?"

"It's as good an excuse as any. Better than most."

Ellenor tried to imagine herself caught up in such a world, where the guillotine would drop when you were twenty-nine years old, so you sucked the marrow out of everything you encountered along the way. Maybe he had a point. But that was no reason for her to join him in this escapade. "Captain Voss will shoot you dead before you're off the ground."

"By the time they wake up and realize what's happening, I'll be in the air."

"What if they post a guard at night to keep watch over the planes?"

"Have they posted one yet?"

She shook her head.

"This can work," he insisted, inching closer to her,

as if the proximity would help convince her. "We'll clear the chocks from the wheels. I'll get in and prime the controls. You'll rotate the propeller—"

"Yes, because I have such experience as a propeller-rotater."

He grinned a little. "I'll teach you. It's actually more difficult than it sounds. You have to do it in such a way that your momentum doesn't tip you forward into the blades when the engine catches."

"I'm liking this scheme more and more every second." She crossed her arms. "Let's say, for argument's sake, that you manage to lift off without getting one of us arrested or killed. Won't the German pilots just jump in their own planes and hunt you down?"

"It will be completely dark. They can't see shit in the dark." He bit his lip and tried again. "I'm sorry. They can't see very well at night."

"And neither can you. How will you find Metz?"

"I'm timing this operation so that the sun will rise about half an hour after I'm in the air. That gives me enough time to avoid pursuit in the darkness, but it also—"

"Also it means you'll soon have light to find your way to Metz."

"One would hope."

She didn't like it. Too many things could go wrong. What if she wasn't able to work the propeller correctly? What if Voss was awake with a loaded gun nearby? What if they didn't believe her when she lied about her role in the theft?

"You're thinking about it," he observed. "You're considering saying yes."

And then Ellenor did something she hadn't done since she was twelve and mad at her cousin Richard for throwing mud at her: she gave Mr. Alec Corbin-Dawes the middle finger.

His eyes widened. He actually pulled back a little in surprise. And then he laughed.

In that laugh, Ellenor saw her decision. Most would think her scandalous for making such a crude gesture—a lady's hands weren't supposed to be capable of such ghastly semaphore—but this was war, and she was, after all, an American. And having been born in a hardscrabble territory before civilized statehood arrived, she recognized the unbelievable daring in his plan and was drawn to it. By helping him, she risked everything. But she was in a toxic mood because of her dead bees and in no condition to listen to reason.

"Teach me about the propeller," she said.

****

When Alec was a boy, he'd met the famous British artist John William Waterhouse. Alec's father, a typesetter at the *Derby Evening Telegraph*, dragged his two children to a public showing of various high-brow paintings, determined to impress upon them the virtues of culture. The artist himself was in attendance, and at some point Alec was shuffled to the front of the small crowd and stood looking up at a man with a pointed black beard.

"I like your painting, sir," Alec mumbled after getting a *say something* poke in the side from his sister.

Waterhouse crouched down and looked him in the eyes. "Which one?"

"The woman in the boat." Alec pointed at *The Lady of Shalott*.

"Ah. Painting that one made me sad," the artist said.

"Why?"

"I'm not certain. I wish I knew. Do you paint, young man?"

Sarah answered for him. "Alec draws."

"Ah, an illustrator. I should have known. You've that look about you." He reached into a coat pocket and produced a graphite pencil. "Here. Use it wisely or foolishly, as it suits you."

"Thank you, sir."

Waterhouse winked.

Now, twenty years later, Alec remembered that pencil as he used a blank page in a beekeeping journal to render a diagram of the Rumpler's engine. Only an inch of the pencil remained, locked away in a lacquered box in his parents' cellar. "Forgive my artistic skills, Miss Jantz. Or the lack thereof, as the case may be."

"You're being modest. And it's 'Ellenor.' Miss Jantz is the sensible woman who teaches Father's children and is learning to cook *Sauerbraten*. She's not the airplane thief."

Alec sketched a side view of the Rumpler's six-cylinder engine to demonstrate how it connected to the propeller, and as he worked, he said her name in his mind: *Ellenor*. He was entrusting his life to her. If she decided he wasn't worth the trouble, she'd inform the Huns of his plot, and he'd be arrested and executed the next morning at dawn. At best, he'd spend the rest of the war inside some medieval-era German prison, shackled to the wall.

"You're actually quite good," Ellenor said as the image came to life on the page.

"Sarah always chided me for wasting my talent."

"Maybe when the war is over…"

"I could become an artist? Give up the glamorous life of a flyboy to take up the brush?"

"Would that be so bad?"

"King George said he'd give Fritz a proper swatting and end the war by Christmas. That was three years ago."

The two of them stood in the supply shed, the door open wide to permit sunlight to illuminate the small space. The journal was splayed open on the lid of a hive box—what Ellenor called a super. Resting in a tub nearby was a brown-yellow mass of unprocessed wax cappings, the remains of Ellenor's most recent honey harvest.

"Here we are, then," he said, indicating the drawing. "This is how air passes through the engine and mixes with the petrol…" He kept it as simple as possible, not because Ellenor couldn't understand it—indeed, she was as astute as anyone he'd ever met—but because his life might depend on the petrol igniting on the first try; it was important they got it right. That done, he discussed the correct form to use when swinging the prop. He took her out of the shed and pantomimed it several times. "Now you try."

She gave him a critical look. "You're certain there's no other way."

"Quite. I'm running out of time. The bombers arrive at Metz in four days."

"I'm not sure how I feel about that."

"What do you mean?"

"Even if you get your sister out of the city in time, others will die."

"There's nothing I can do about that."

"Those are factory workers, not soldiers."

"I didn't authorize the attack. Those decisions are made far above my rank."

"So you'll whisk your sister away and allow everyone else to be killed?"

Alec rubbed his face. He needed a shave. He needed a shave and a fast plane and a ticket for two on a steamer back home. "Look, it's like this. I'm no proponent of killing anyone, but if killing has to be done, then we might as well do it to the Boche. They started this infernal war, remember? So if the Allied Powers say we've got to kill Germans to defend France and Belgium, then I'm not going to ask them to call off an aerial raid that will save the lives of our boys by cutting off supplies to the enemy. That raid is going to happen, regardless of what I say or do. And maybe Sarah will get lucky and be at home or at the market when those nasty Breguet bombers dump their payload, but maybe not. Do I feel bad for the factory workers? I suppose I do. But they are not Sarah. They're not my sister. So bugger them."

If he'd expected a dramatic reaction from Ellenor, she again surprised him. Instead of arguing, instead of challenging him with those emerald eyes of hers, she glanced back in the direction of the drawing just inside the shed door. "This plane is capable of doing what you need it to do?"

"They call it a Rumpler. There's a seat for an observer or gunner directly behind the pilot, and that means I've got a chance. I can't get Sarah out of Germany in a car or smuggle her out in the back of a lorry, and we damn sure can't make it on foot. It may be an ungainly beast, but the Rumpler has enough range to get me to Metz and then carry the two of us back across the Hindenburg Line."

"What if the gas tank isn't full?"

"Gas?"

"Fuel. *Petrol*. How do you know there'll be enough?"

He hadn't considered it, and that made him chuckle grimly. "Damn." He shook his head at his own folly, then shrugged. "Let's just hope those Hun flyboys keep their crates topped off, shall we?" He waited for her response. What was she thinking? She was the key to the entire half-baked operation, but if he hoped to see commitment in her eyes, he was disappointed. He had a sudden, curious desire to sit down on the grass and talk to her, because after tomorrow morning in the pre-dawn hours, he'd never see her again. He'd fly away, deeper into Germany, and then—God willing—back to France. He would never know if the German officers believed Ellenor's false explanation for the theft. He'd never know if she ever discovered what ill had befallen her poor bees.

"Why are you looking at me like that?" she asked.

"I'm not sure. I wonder about you."

"Wonder what?"

"Why you've agreed to help me."

"It's not too late for me to change my mind. I still might, you know."

"I don't think you will."

Ellenor moved her hand in a way that said, *You never know*. "I hope this sister of yours is worth it. You tell her that Ellenor from New Mexico says hello."

"I certainly shall."

"Now show me again what I'm supposed to do so I don't get my head cut off by this damned propeller. You wouldn't want that on your conscience, now, would you?"

Smiling, he showed her.

Chapter Nine

Ellenor returned to the estate just before dinner and took her place at the expansive table, seated directly across from *Hauptmann* Gustov Voss. Between them was a beef *rouladen* in thick brown gravy, local chanterelle mushrooms, and a tureen of fatty vegetable broth and bread for dipping into it. The table was set with some of the expensive china; nothing but the best for their guests.

Father stood and prayed.

Ellenor wasn't Lutheran. In fact, she wasn't much of anything, as least as far as religion was concerned. Her papa had taught her to depend on herself. Salvation, he said, could be found first in your own two hands. As a girl, Ellenor and her family lived miles away from the nearest church, and her papa wasn't about to load them all into a buckboard and snap the reins every Sunday just to hear an overeducated preacher from back east talk about the wisdom of Solomon, who supposedly had seven hundred wives.

Solomon sounds like he couldn't keep his privates in his pants, she recalled Papa saying.

Ellenor bit down on her smile as Father concluded saying grace and took his seat with a pop of the crisp linen napkin in his lap.

Everyone spoke at once, carrying on conversations around the table. Ellenor loved this about Father; he didn't glower; he didn't bolt his children to rigid manners; he didn't impose his will on anyone, at least not with any great amount of pressure. He adored his family and the life he'd made. He valued robust friendship and found the idea of a quiet dinner table to be terrifying. So everyone, young and old, enjoyed each other and the food.

Ellenor glanced at the grandfather clock with its massive pendulum. In less than twelve hours, she would touch the plane's propeller for real and execute the movement she'd been taught. And with that, Lieutenant Alec Corbin-Dawes of the Royal Flying Corps would be on his way, a dream she would occasionally have years from now until the memory faded.

"...unless Miss Jantz is still armed with her butcher's knife."

She blinked and saw Voss smiling at her playfully. "I'm sorry. I was—"

"Woolgathering? Yes, I'm prone to that myself. I was telling Father that I'd discovered his cache of wine but was swearing to abide by the rules of its guardian." He tipped his glass of 1898 Fiano at her.

"I'm afraid I make for a poor guardian. I'm more concerned with teaching Karl and Truda to conjugate verbs."

"A skill that some of my squad have yet to master."

He said this loudly enough that the other members of the *Jasta*, seated around the table among the family and staff, grunted in agreement or gave him a thumbs-up. They were a well-mannered and impeccably groomed lot of boys who thought they were men. The one seated next to Karl could barely eat for all the questions he was asked about his aircraft and his missions. He seemed happy to tell his stories to such an eager listener.

"Personally, I enjoyed my language studies," Voss continued, spearing a slice of beef. "I didn't mind the Latin lessons, nor the Greek, but the little bit of Russian they wanted me to learn was akin to torture. They said it was important to read Tolstoy in the man's original tongue. I'd rather muck out stables all day and spend all night cleaning the shovels."

Father nodded his agreement. "Russian can be challenging. It is the language of a cold and calculating people. And since their emperor abdicated a few months ago, the entire country is one wiggle away from anarchy." He gestured with his fork. "Miss Jantz here is quite adept at languages herself."

"Is she?"

Ellenor shrugged with one shoulder as she sipped her soup.

Father looked at Voss. "Where would you place her accent?" He turned to Ellenor. "Mind providing a sample, Miss Jantz?"

An uncomfortable warmth spread across Ellenor's back. Her dress suddenly felt sticky. This was not where she wanted the conversation to dwell. "I, um…" She quoted her favorite line from the philosopher Kant: "'Live your life as though your every act were to become a universal law.'"

"Hmmm. Do I detect a bit of a Lorraine patois?"

Father laughed, his infectious baritone ringing out across the marbled hall. "She has you fooled, sir. Ellenor Jantz is a Yankee, born and bred."

Voss blinked as if he'd misheard. "You're *American*?"

"Guilty as charged," she said in English. She switched back to German and added, "I hope you don't hold that against me."

"You've no accent at all. You sound like a native."

"I seem to have a knack for the language."

"To say the least." He put down his drink and laced his fingers in front of him. "How did an American woman come to be all the way over here in these humble farmlands?"

"You're not the first person to ask that. But the answer isn't very exciting, I'm afraid." She didn't tell him about the dandelion; she didn't relate the story she'd told to Alec. Instead she said, "I had few opportunities back home. A woman in the American West is often expected to perform a role to which I am not particularly well suited."

This seemed to please him. "You surprise me, Miss Jantz. My men refer to me as the Grizzled in part because I'm not often surprised."

My surprises have only just begun, she thought, avoiding another peek at the clock.

Voss was about to say something else when little Truda started singing at the request of one of the airmen, and seconds later the entire table was clapping along, in between bites of beef-wrapped bacon and mustard sauce.

Ellenor didn't allow herself the luxury of relaxing, though she felt like slumping back in her chair. The last thing she wanted was the undue attention of Gustov Voss, as shrewd a fox hunter as they came. She'd sat down to dinner with the intention of passing the time as invisibly as possible, like a woman near the exit door at the back of a crowded theater, yet somehow she'd tumbled into the center of the scene.

Things got better after that. Voss apparently forgot about her. He and Father fell into a complex discussion of the latest war offensive and how it was impacted by the increasing use of radio signals as a means of communicating across the battlefield. Observers in floating dirigibles were now able to relay troop movements to artillery emplacements on the ground. The other men of the *Jasta*, immaculate in their uniforms of dark gray with red piping, got up from the table and demonstrated flying maneuvers, much to the delight of the children. Ellenor watched them. They seemed too fit and full of good manners and jubilation to face death so often as they did. They spoke reverently of fallen Oswald Boelcke, the Saxon ace with forty kills who'd died last autumn when his Albatros collided with one of his own squadron members over Bapaume. He was only twenty-five.

Ellenor, a virtual spinster at twenty-seven, felt ancient among them. What had she done in her life that would ever be a tale by which to entertain children when she was gone? Other than mastering a foreign language, she was nothing but a displaced American, an adequate teacher, and a mediocre beekeeper.

And a virtuoso propeller-turner.

Well, that remained to be seen.

When one of the fearless young flyers asked for a tour of the residence and offered his arm, she surprised the hell out of herself by saying yes.

****

Alec waited for nightfall doing something he'd never imagined: he sat among bees.

Donning the pith helmet and its protective veil,

71

along with a pair of gloves slightly too small for him, he walked up the hill from his hideout in the shed. Ellenor had told him that honey bees meant no harm.

What about the harm they intend when they sting the shit out of you? he'd asked.

That's done only in self-defense.

So if I don't jostle them or swat at them or look at them funny, they'll leave me alone?

When a bee stings you, she dies. So yes, they'll leave you alone.

Alec thought about that as he shifted a bit on the grass, ten feet from the two remaining colonies. Bees formed a cloud around their stacked boxes, alighting on the landing boards with colored puffs of pollen stuck to their legs. Stinging was suicide, the last defense to protect the clan. Knowing that, Alec felt at peace, much as he did when patrolling the clouds at ten thousand feet. He thought of his fearsome S.E.5, which he'd dubbed The Dragon. When he was safe inside her belly and the ground so far away, it looked pretend, and he entered a kind of meditative state. He understood how the bees could do that for Ellenor. You learned to be the calm core in the middle of a storm.

Darkness dropped its cloak across the sky.

Alec lifted the veil over the brim of his helmet. He watched the bees disappear into the narrow slot that was the portal to their hot, dark world. Ellenor had told him the bees used the vibration of their bodies to keep the interior temperature at a constant ninety-five degrees Fahrenheit, a deep, murky heat. Nighttime forced them inside. Soon it was too dark for both Alec and the bees, and the only thing visible was starlight.

He sat and thought and waited for the hours to

pass. He lay on his back and stared at all the silver shapes in the sky.

When it was time, he stood up and took one long, emancipating piss before leaving the shed behind forever. He picked up a full canteen along the way, as well as a small tin of dried venison and nuts—a light meal to enjoy during his hopefully uneventful flight to Metz. He would be flying a German bomber in German skies and anticipated no trouble.

He made his way in the dark, careful to remain on the path.

Halfway down the hill, with a mile to go before he reached the villa and its support buildings, he realized he still wore the pith helmet. He took it off and studied it as he continued his hike, his eyes fully adjusted and making the most of the meager moon. Fashioned of Indian cork covered in khaki-colored canvas, it was the kind of lid worn when slicing through jungles or shooting at tigers from afar. Ellenor had looked charming in it, the heroine of her own dime store novel, *The Girl in the Pith Helmet*. Except she was no girl. She drove automobiles and shot fallen pilots with bolt-action rifles. She was a woman, make no mistake.

Alec tapped the helmet against his leg as he walked. He'd give it back to her soon, though he would ask to keep the gloves so that his fingers wouldn't freeze on the stick. He had no bees to keep the cockpit warm.

The middle of his left hand was still a bright circle of pain. A little something to remember her by.

He quickened his pace. The ache had left his muscles. Bruises remained, but his body came alive, rejuvenated by the task before him. He felt the tingle in his gut again, the very feeling he experienced before taking The Dragon out on patrol. That tingle meant you could be killed. It kept you on edge, kept you sharp, kept your head panning left and right to catch an ambush before it was sprung. That tingle was the combination of excitement and fear, and it was what made airmen on either side of the Front so different from the mud-crunching infantry below. A soldier on the ground charged a machine-gun nest to beat the devil at his own game; a pilot wanted to know what it felt like to be a devil himself.

A hundred yards from the barley field where the Fokkers waited, flanking that lone bomber, Alec dropped into a crouch, half-smiling as he went.

Chapter Ten

In the summer of 1917, whether one lived in Germany or in any other civilized nation, the height of women's fashion was decidedly *not* a coarse black sweater and Wellington boots.

Ellenor examined herself in the looking glass. The sweater's sleeves were long enough to cover most of her hands, exposing only her fingers, and its rolled neckline cupped her face just below her chin. It was made of sheep's wool and stained black with plant dyes. She'd bound her hair behind her back; God forbid it got caught up in the propeller.

Sure about this? she asked herself.

"Not at all, thanks." Certain highbrows claimed that women should not be seen in trousers, but Ellenor had always found them far more practical when working outdoors. You certainly didn't want bees hunting forage under your skirt. Her calf-high leather boots were years out of style but weatherproof, dependable, and—most importantly—comfortable. Her ensemble was utilitarian, but it fit her well, conforming to the natural curves of her body.

She checked the porcelain-faced clock on the mantel in her room.

Working by the light of a beeswax candle she'd made herself, she packed a small satchel for Alec. She'd washed his clothing—he'd been wearing Josef's shirt and pants since that first day in the barn—and now folded it neatly at the bottom of the bag. She followed this with his flight goggles, a package of Nil cigarettes, a blanket, a few red phosphorus matches, and his blood-stained blue scarf. She'd wanted to include a flask of whiskey but had been afraid of being seen sneaking into the wine cellar.

That done, she waited and paced.

The entire house was asleep. She'd spent a good hour in light conversation with one of the German flyers, a nineteen-year-old from Cologne named Otto. He clearly wanted to seduce her, and in these pursuits he wasn't entirely inept but certainly inexperienced. Ellenor didn't hold it against him. Airmen were spontaneous and eloquent and exquisitely aware of death. They made women feel good for a night or two, and then they went off and died by the hundreds, many of them still smelling of perfume.

"We'll chat again tomorrow," Ellenor had told him, and Otto played the part of the gentleman so well that she found it remarkable that he was fighting in the same war as men who ate cold beets in a muddy trench and shaved their heads to rid themselves of lice.

It was time.

She reviewed her assignment one last time in her mind, the lifting of her arms, the bending of her back, the straining of her muscles as she pulled. Alec depended on her to help him save his sister from the bombs, and that dependence was exhilarating; she had value beyond teaching Karl and Truda to speak English. She could rescue someone—at least indirectly. Maybe one day Alec would be able to write to her on clean British stationary and let her know that he and Sarah had made it home.

Arms, back, pull!

She removed her boots and walked in stocking feet to the narrow door in the kitchen. Once there, having safely crossed the house in silence, she put her boots back on, chewed on her bottom lip for a few moments, and then let herself outside.

The world was mostly quiet. Insects chirped and buzzed. The ceramic wind chime on the barn awning tinkled in a breeze so faint it was little more than a whisper. At four-thirty in the morning, the estate grounds felt empty, as no kerosene lamp burned in a window and no oven had yet been stoked to life for morning muffins. The animals slept soundly in their pens.

Ellenor struck off toward the grain fields. If her boots left tracks in the dew, it was too dark to see them.

Arms, back, pull!

She knew her escape route. As soon as the plane's engine caught, she'd shout a last goodbye to Alec and then move quickly to the far side of the barn, keeping that rambling structure between her and anyone who emerged from the house in response to the sudden noise. From there, she'd be able to return to her room either through the kitchen door or—if that way was blocked by a sleepy-eyed occupant—she'd use the glass door at the garden. She'd left it unlocked just to be sure.

Her eyes made sense of the shadows. The silhouettes of the planes appeared.

She'd memorized their positions so as to move directly to the one that Alec called the Rumpler. She touched them as she passed, these unlikely inventions that allowed man at last to leave the ground after so many failed attempts by inventors of the previous century. She'd witnessed her first airplane at a public demonstration four years ago, and like everyone else in the crowd, she'd had to force herself to exhale. That's how fantastic it all was, this business of sailing the sky. It had seemed like part of a fairy tale then. The war had seized that fairy tale and turned it into a weapon.

Smelling the castor oil, the axle grease, and the wax on the wings, she reached the largest of the planes just as a voice said, "Fancy meeting you here."

Alec sat on the Rumpler's lower wing, between the taut wires that held the two decks in place. Ellenor drew closer so she could see his face. "You were worried I wouldn't come?"

"I've heard it said that modern women have a tendency to change their minds."

"Women have always changed their minds," she said. "But only recently have we been permitted to get away with it."

"And soon you'll even be voting in political elections, by the looks of it."

She shrugged, near enough to him that he could see her expression of disinterest in the matter. "I'm no suffragette, but I wouldn't mind having a say in what fools are elected to govern us."

He smiled. "If you're looking for fools, search no further." He slid off the wing. "Here, I brought you something."

She accepted the pith helmet. "You're welcome to keep it, if you think it would help."

"You'll need it for the bees. But if you're willing to part with these gloves…"

"Of course. They're yours. And here are your

clothes and a few other things I packed." She handed him the satchel, then hung the helmet down her back by its leather chinstrap.

"Thank you," he said. "Really. For all of this. You're taking a serious risk for a bloke you barely know."

"Maybe I'm doing it for the bloke's sister. I'm sure she's the more sensible twin."

"That goes without saying. Well, then. We've about thirty minutes until daybreak. Shall we?"

Ellenor gathered a breath, let it out, and nodded.

Alec went over it one final time as he tightened the goatskin gloves over each individual finger and buttoned up his coat. Ellenor never looked away from his eyes as he spoke. Should she hug him goodbye? She hardly knew him. When he was finished, she resisted the urge and offered her hand instead.

He took her hand gently, leaned toward her, and kissed her on the forehead. "It's been a pleasure being shot in the hand by you, Miss Jantz."

She swatted him lightly on the arm. "Tell your sister I said hello."

He held his smile in place, nodded firmly, and then turned and pulled the wedge-shaped chocks from the wheels. Nothing but hundreds of yards of open ground lay in front of the Rumpler's nose. Once the engine caught, the plane would begin rolling forward. He dropped the satchel into the observer's seat, moving differently than he had a few minutes before; a new energy infused him and gave him grace. He'd probably already spent time checking the integrity of the plane's many components, so with the chocks gone, he climbed onto the wing and then lowered himself into the man-sized hole that was the cockpit, a British pilot at the controls of a German plane.

Ellenor went to the propeller.

Alec had already turned it several times—something about settling the oil or positioning the cylinders—and now one long wooden blade waited almost parallel with the ground. He'd placed an overturned Red Cross crate to give her the height she needed, and now she stepped up on it and placed both hands along the blade's top edge. The wood was smooth and thick.

Arms, back, pull!

She waited for him to say it, counting her breaths, and then he did, his voice carrying clearly to her in the dark: "Contact."

She heaved down on the propeller.

Nothing happened.

She did it again, repeating the motion. The engine ticked as things moved inside of it, but that was all. She heard Alec adjusting levers or handles or—

"Contact," he said again.

Wishing she would have hugged him, Ellenor heaved.

The engine barked hard three times. Ellenor leaped back, hands going instinctively to cover her ears...

The plane sputtered. The propeller turned twice more and stopped.

She looked in the direction of the house. No one was there.

"*Contact.*"

"I'm trying, damn it." She got back on the Red Cross crate, grabbed the stupid propeller, and yanked downward with all the strength she could muster.

The engine snarled, stuttered…and then banged out a long, unsteady rhythm so loud that it made Ellenor wince. She hurried backward, and a moment later, lamplight appeared in one of the house's upper windows.

The plane barely moved, its cadence not yet established. The engine sped up, the propeller churning the air madly. With agonizing slowness, the aircraft crept forward.

Ellenor looked back and forth from plane to house. Another light winked on. The din was unbelievable. All of that noise, and yet the plane was barely moving. Ellenor thought about jumping close and trying to push the thing along—

And then another sound, somehow even louder than the howling motor, cracked the starry night a few feet away. A full second passed before Ellenor realized what was happening.

She was being shot at.

She stared at the house and saw a man framed there against the glare of kerosene maps. He was nothing but a figure cut from black crepe, a man-shape with one arm extended. A muzzle-flash appeared in his hand.

A bullet struck the ground in front of her.

All sense of place and time abandoned her. The fear was so delicate, so weightless, that it crystallized her, so that she felt as if she might break into frail pieces and float away. Someone was trying to kill her.

She turned and ran beside the plane.

Two hundred yards separated the makeshift airfield from the shooter at the house, no easy shot at night for even a trained marksman. The bullets flew by her, aiming for the engine racket. By now, some of the

German airmen were running toward her, barefoot but armed. This was not how it was supposed to happen. They'd reacted too quickly. The plane had taken too long to move. Hell, it was barely moving now.

A bullet whined a few inches overhead.

Ellenor ran with everything she had. Terror squeezed a tiny sound from her throat, but she couldn't hear it. Her heart tried to punch through her ribs...

"Get in!"

She heard him but didn't know what to do. She pumped her arms up and down as she ran, her boots biting into the soft soil, the pith helmet banging against her back. Tears glazed her eyes and streaked into her hair from the wind.

"Get in, goddammit!"

The plane was starting to pull away. Alec leaned halfway from his hole, waving his arm at her.

More bullets lanced the darkness.

"Get in or die!"

Ellenor latched onto his voice like a drowning woman reaching for a rope. She veered toward the rolling plane, almost cut in half by the wing. Grunting for air, she lunged upward, grabbing the rim of the observer's seat and hauling herself up with undiscovered strength. Alec leaned on the throttle, almost causing her to lose her grip. Frantically, with panic nearly blinding her, she dropped onto the hard, round seat behind him.

The Rumpler jumped and jolted over the field, building speed by the second.

Ellenor choked down each new breath. Eyes mashed shut, she leaned forward as best she could, arms locked around herself. The engine roared in one long, protracted sound, the air whistling through the wires. She bit down forcefully to keep her teeth from banging.

And then, abruptly, the world dissolved.

Ellenor's stomach performed a weird little wobble inside her, and a sensation she'd never known coursed through her body. The knocking and jostling of the wheels vanished at once, and a strange force pushed her back against her seat. She opened her eyes to see herself pointed straight at the stars.

I'm flying.

She looked over the side. It was too dark to see anything. Was the field of barley down there somewhere? The vibrating terror of moments before was wiped away by the tranquility of disconnection. The earth had let go of Ellenor Jantz. For the first time in her life, she escaped gravity, and now she rushed through the unfettered wind.

"Are you all right?"

Some distant part of her knew that Alec had shouted these words over his shoulder, but she was too awestruck to respond. To go from almost dying to sweeping skyward left her unable to reply. Speaking actual human words felt like a violation.

"*Ellenor, are you hurt?*"

She had nothing to say. She felt like weeping in relief and laughing in girlish delight. She reached forward, found his shoulder, and squeezed.

He patted her hand, then flew them high and far toward the east and whatever the coming dawn might bring.

Part Two
Pursuit

Chapter Eleven

Gustov Voss stood barefoot in the field and listened to the stolen machine fly far beyond his reach. Panting for breath, he raised his pistol and fired the last of its eight rounds in the direction of the departing sound, purely from frustration rather than intent, as the Luger's effective range was no more than fifty meters. He kept his arm extended, glaring along the barrel at the stars, trying to understand what had just occurred.

"Captain?"

Twenty minutes ago, he'd awakened peacefully and made his way from his borrowed bedroom through the dark house to the kitchen. He prepared a kettle for tea. Then the noise alerted him, and he'd retrieved his gun. Now he stood hard-jawed and breathing heavily with an empty sidearm pointed at an equally empty sky.

"Captain Voss?"

He lowered the gun, finger still on the trigger. He wore a long nightshirt and trousers and nothing else. He'd just raced across an airfield as one of the craft in his care was taken from him, leaving him with dirt between his toes.

What had just happened? *How* had it happened?

It angered him to look away from the sky, to admit that he'd been outwitted, robbed. The sound of the vanished plane was not even that of a buzzing insect. A second later it was entirely gone.

Gustov gathered himself, turned, and said, "There is a teapot on the stove, Lieutenant Mier. See that it is removed before the water boils away and ruins the kettle."

"Of course, sir."

That helped. Gustov restored order to himself with that simple command. Mier trotted away, his own sidearm still in his hand, its magazine depleted.

Resisting the urge to cast another angry glare at the vacant sky, Gustov stalked to the remaining planes. Swinging lanterns revealed more of his men, all in various stages of undress. Ignoring them for a moment, Gustov inventoried the squadron, noting instantly that all eleven Fokkers were accounted for. The Rumpler C.IV was gone. Over fifteen hundred kilos of plane and munitions had been spirited away.

Gustov's rage was not really rage. He realized it was embarrassment. Thank Christ the men could barely see his face in the dark. Without looking at any of them, he said, "Does anyone hold any information that I do not possess regarding this incident?"

Almost at once they replied, "No, sir."

He held very still, making random, baseless guesses at to what might have happened. They were too far from the Front to be the target of enemy provocateurs. Weren't they? And if a trained pilot had gotten drunk and fancied a midnight flight, why not choose one of the unbeatable Fokker triplanes?

"I want six of you in the air immediately. Though our craft just departed on an eastward heading, they might very well change direction. Split up. Fly at different elevations. Cover as much airspace as you can. Go now."

They quickly chose who among them would go; Gustov always encouraged them to make choices rather than blindly follow orders. To those who remained, he said, "Assemble the household. Everyone. But do it politely."

In a moment, he was alone.

An earlier, pre-war version of himself would have chuckled at his plight. He'd always been a jovial youth who enjoyed horsemanship and hunting and anything in skirts. He'd intended to pursue a career in finance, if he was ever forced to give up gallivanting and put a roof over a woman's head. But then a Serbian assassin had put a slug into the Archduke of Austria, the world lit itself on fire, and six months later Gustov learned to fly.

He turned and walked purposefully to the house.

While the others gathered in the drawing room, he attended to his appearance, dressing in the full service regalia of a German officer of the Air Force. He donned his gray M1910 field tunic. He buttoned its high collar, where double silver braids of metal flashed on dark velvet. With the help of a mirror, he straightened the tunic's shoulder boards, each outlined in red piping and featuring a gilt-metal winged propeller device in the center. He inspected his wool field cap for lint, cleaning its black visor on his palm. He carried it with him as he went downstairs.

As soon as he entered the drawing room, he knew he would need to move everyone outside. The chamber was appointed in stained walnut with brass accents. The writing desk was a great bear of a thing, a slab of wood on legs carved with an aggressive Etruscan motif, with a bust of some honored ancestor or perhaps a Roman senator resting sternly on one corner. Due to that desk and the fine cabinetry around it, there simply wasn't enough space, as the aircraft mechanics, cooks, couriers, and valets had arrived last night, tripling the property's population.

With assistance from Father, they herded the sleepy crowd outside, where a thin band of light appeared in the east, casting pale light over the lawn. Even Karl and Truda were here, the latter slumped against Father's shoulder while the former looked around expectantly with his hair rampant on his head. The first birds had awakened. The air smelled crisp and faintly of apples.

Gustov took his place at the front, facing them, hat on his head at the prescribed angle. His men stood at attention; the civilians blinked and looked around, wondering why they'd been summoned. Gustov loved them all, these hardworking, scrappy men and women who cooked good food and raised respectful children. This is why he fought, not for the government in Berlin—a congregation of craggy old misers who provided inadequate boots for their soldiers—but for people who whistled, people who chopped cabbage, people with heart.

Yet…one of them might know something they'd yet to share.

"My deepest apologies," he began, his voice carrying easily across the morning field. "As you are no doubt aware by now, one of our flying machines was taken from us within the last half hour. Quite…*daringly,* an unknown person absconded with property not their own. I will be frank with you, my friends, and admit that I have not the faintest notion as to how or why this happened. And so I beseech you, please, if you have any insight into this matter, come forward now."

His men did not move, iron rods in their backs. The mechanics and the rest of the enlisted men did the same, though many of them were unshaven, with dirt under their nails. The household staff and family members, not bound by rank, traded confused glances, shook their heads, or shrugged.

Gustov had anticipated this precise reaction, and so he leveled his gaze on individual faces, rapidly moving from one to the next, depending on his instincts as a hunter. He thought he noticed something almost immediately, but he needed to be sure.

"Do not be afraid," he told them. "I have complete faith in your good intentions. Please." He spread his hands, palms out, in a gesture that invited cooperation.

One of the women, the cook, looked around as if seeking something.

"Madam?" Gustov smiled. "Dagmar, isn't it?"

Everyone looked at her. She nodded.

"Madam, I find myself rather desperately in need of your assistance. What do you know that can help me?"

"Nothing, sir. I swear it. I was…I was just looking for…"

"For whom?"

"For Miss Jantz, sir."

Gustov studied the small crowd again. Miss Jantz? How had he overlooked her absence? "The American is missing," he said, as much to himself as to his audience. "She's not in her room?"

"She is not, Captain," Schmit confirmed, never breaking attention. "I checked every room myself to make sure all had heard the summons."

Gustov didn't know what to make of it. Ellenor Jantz, as alluring as she might have been, had not stolen a bomber. "Has anyone seen her since dinner last night?"

No one had.

Again he watched their faces. With every passing second, his suspicions deepened. He kept his apprehension from his voice when he said, "I find it difficult to imagine that Miss Jantz is actually a man in disguise who was trained by French intelligence to infiltrate a German farm on the small chance that an air squadron would be stationed there so he could steal an observation plane from among a group of freshly painted Fokkers." He smiled a little; that's how strange it sounded. "Don't you all agree?"

His eyes settled on the tall, rangy stablemaster. "You, sir. I'm sorry, but I can't recall your name."

"Um…I am Josef. Josef Rosenstein."

"Of course. I won't forget again. I couldn't help but notice that you seem troubled, Mr. Rosenstein. The look on your face…I can't quite read it. Could you enlighten me?"

Josef turned his cowboy hat over and over in his hands. His friends looked at him askance.

"Mr. Rosenstein? It seems you have us all at a disadvantage. Can you share?"

"It's that, uh…Ellenor…well, she was…helping someone."

Gustov moved closer. The crowd parted. He stood before Josef and extended his hand. He'd always liked shaking hands, clasping another's fingers, making contact. Some days that simple act seemed like the last civilized gesture in the world.

Josef, surprised, shook vigorously.

"Call me Gustov, and I shall call you Joe."

Josef nodded.

"Joe, I am at a loss. Ellenor did not steal that plane."

"No, sir."

Gustov dismissed the *sir* with a wave. "You're ten years my senior, Joe. Please call me by the name my mother gave me."

"All right."

"So. Ellenor. Our clever American. She was helping someone, you say?"

"Yes, Gustov."

For some reason, Gustov recalled the line Ellenor had quoted at supper to demonstrate her command of German: *Live your life as though your every act were to become a universal law*. Gustov's universal law was honor. What was Ellenor's?

He leaned so close that only Josef could hear: "Helping whom?"

After a moment's hesitation, Josef whispered the answer in his ear.

Chapter Twelve

Alec nudged the rudder bar with his foot, putting the plane into a smooth, arcing turn. The morning sun waited just ahead, huge but not quite warm, at least not at eight thousand feet above the ground. The engine produced a constant, reassuring hum. Safe behind his goggles, he watched the clouds break apart like things made of gossamer threads. The ground winked by in little patches of brown and green, visible only when he waggled his wings and got a glance over the side.

His plan, of course, was ruined. He tried not to think about that. Not right now. Ellenor was supposed to be distant miles behind him, quietly going about her life as she'd done before she found him crumpled in the wildflowers on the hill. But wasn't it a German field marshal who warned that no plan survived contact with the enemy? Alec remembered hearing such a thing during his officer training, and it certainly applied now. Enemy bullets had changed everything, and now what in the bloody hell was he supposed to do?

"Just fly, old boy," he said to himself.

He flew.

The Rumpler impressed him. Seated below the upper wing, with the engine directly in front of him, he felt a sense of stability that he'd not experienced in lighter craft. The gauges were labeled in German on stamped metal plates, but Alec didn't need to read them, as their function was immediately clear: oil pressure, compass, airspeed, altimeter. He knew them by heart, and he felt a kinship with the Boche pilot who'd most recently occupied this seat. The two of them would never meet. But they both appreciated this small space, where you barely had the room to shift your arse on the seat, yet at the same time, you commanded the pitiful ground below. At any moment you could fall upon the pointless people there and scatter them with your guns.

So caught up was he in his reverie that he almost cried out in surprise when a hand clutched his shoulder.

Ellenor's shout issued from immediately behind him: "*I. Am freezing. To death.*"

Shit, he hadn't even considered her comfort. He nodded hastily to acknowledge her, then eased the plane into a gentle descent, the wires humming between the wings. The land came into focus swiftly, the farms, the fields, the country roads connecting them. Miles of rural Germany lay before them; the streams, plowed fields, and villages looked more like a painting from this distance than real life. Alec brought the plane down even lower, the air warming as he dropped. Though wooded areas were prominent, plenty of open spaces offered impromptu airfields. Alec had memorized the maps and knew his way to Metz, more or less, but he saw no prominent landmarks. Lifting off in the dark had thwarted potential pursuers but removed him from his original flight plan.

He chose a clear pasture with a few head of livestock at the near end but nothing else other than an inviting stretch of native grasses for at least five hundred yards. The morning sun turned that grass to a pale, perfect green.

He dumped his speed and then cut off his engine entirely so that he glided those last few feet before his wheels bumped the ground.

No landing field—improvised or intentional—was ever as smooth as it looked from the air. Holes and ridges abounded, drumming into Alec's tailbone and knocking him back and forth into the leather-wrapped rim of his hole. He'd learned to absorb much of the force in his shoulders, holding a hunched position while the plane bounded across the ground. He only hoped that Ellenor wasn't having too poor a go of it behind him.

Momentum carried the Rumpler along, high grasses whipping at the wheels. The back end of the crate touched down, the landing skid creating a jagged wake of weeds and dirt. As friction devoured their momentum, Alec tugged his goggles off and let them hang around his neck. Finally the plane stopped, the prop coming to a standstill like a broken clock.

He twisted in his seat. "Hanging in there?"

She gave him a half-hearted thumbs-up but said nothing. She had a blanket wrapped around her and her pith helmet pulled down over her face.

Alec stood, thrilled and angry at the same time. He needed to reassess the situation but wasn't sure where to begin. Hauling himself up and out, he noticed something on his seat that he hadn't seen when climbing inside in the dark. Someone had stitched a single word into the leather: HILDEGARD.

He offered both hands to Ellenor. "Let me help you get out."

She said nothing, but she grabbed onto him and

allowed herself to be hauled from the observer's seat, a machine gun mounted directly behind her. He assisted her to the ground, and then for several awkward seconds the two of them stood there, one in beekeeping gloves and the other in a helmet that hid her eyes.

Not knowing what else to do, Alec said, "Our bus here has a name."

Moments passed, and finally she replied: "I don't know what that means."

"Bus means plane. Ours is apparently named Hildegard."

"I thought it was called a Rumpler."

"Well, I was mistaken. She's a female, it would seem. And probably once loved by her pilot and observer before she was taken as plunder. Come on. Let's get you in the sun and warmed up."

They left the plane's shadow but took only a few steps before Ellenor stopped. She took off the helmet and let it fall. Her hair was wild around her shoulders. "What have I done? Everything is lost. I can't go back now."

"They would have killed you had you stayed."

"You don't know that for sure."

"They were firing blindly in the dark, quite willing to murder anyone near this plane. Yes, I'm afraid you would have died. I'm glad you got in."

"But…it wasn't supposed to happen like that."

"Such is daily life in a war."

"And what am I supposed to do now? Walk back and beg for forgiveness?"

"I shouldn't think that's possible."

"Of course it's not possible. Everything I had just a few hours ago…it's gone. That was my life. I agreed to help you, and before I even knew what was happening, it was over."

"And before *I* even knew what was happening, you took the seat that is intended for Sarah. I can't fly both of you out of Germany."

"I don't want to leave Germany. This is my home."

"Well, I've spoiled home for you, it seems. Sorry, but there was no way for me to—"

"I know, I know, two people are required to start your damn plane. You're welcome, by the way." She sat down on the ground, forearms on her knees.

Alec pinched that place between his eyes and rubbed. The sun rose behind him, revealing dots of lavender and white, a constellation of color across the pasture. He knelt and picked one of the flowers. The French squadron would fill the sky above Metz in three days, at approximately 0400 in the morning. And Sarah's seat in Hildegard had been taken by a woman who didn't even want it.

"They're called *die Akelei*," Ellenor said.

He turned. "I'm sorry?"

"That flower in your hand. It's a Columbine."

"Ah. I'm assuming you know this because of the bees."

"I know everything because of the bees." She hooked her errant hair behind her ear. Her black sweater would warm her quickly in the sun.

Alec felt like challenging her because—even though it wasn't her fault—she was now an impediment. At the same time, it was his nature to try and lighten the mood. One of his mates back at the aerodrome had said all that optimism was bound to be his undoing. "I bet those bees didn't teach you the meaning of *cootie carnival*."

She finally looked at him. "War slang, I assume?"

"Indeed. A cootie carnival is an act of hygiene in which a soldier attempts to rid himself lice."

"That is...disturbing."

"Soldiers do so love a silly phrase. For instance, if you're said to be 'fighting on the cognac front,' that means you're drunk. And those metal struts there on Hildegard's undercarriage where the bombs are, that's called an egg basket."

"I see."

"How about a *honey wagon*?"

"I'm afraid to ask."

"It's an overflowing French manure cart."

"That's disgusting."

He smiled without humor. "Men are a disgusting lot. Pigs, really, every bleeding one of us."

She was silent for a moment, then: "I'm sorry I've ruined things for you."

He stood up, flower in hand. "*Ruined* remains to be seen. In the meantime, I don't know what to do with you."

"I think I have to go back to Father's house."

"You'll be arrested."

"What choice do I have?"

"You abetted an enemy soldier. They will not take that lightly. Considering you're a woman, I doubt they will go so far as to beat the truth out of you, but it still won't be pretty. They'll see it as espionage, gender notwithstanding."

"Espionage? That's preposterous."

"They'll lock you up, preposterous or not. You are not a German citizen. You're an undocumented foreign operative who will spend the remainder of this endless war in a prison cell in Nuremberg or Heidelberg or some other bloody damn *berg*."

"I'm nobody's operative."

"An accidental operative, then."

"I shouldn't have gotten into the plane. I could have turned around and explained to them—"

"You would have been shot, in the dark." He went to her and looked down at where she sat in the grass. "That kit you brought along for me. Yesterday you mentioned a blanket and cigarettes. I'm assuming this is the blanket here, so I'm wondering about the tobacco. If we're going to be miserable, we might as well be miserable and smoke."

"It's in the bag."

He flicked the Columbine away and mounted Hildegard's wing. The observer's seat—a wooden stool on a swivel—was surrounded by a steel ring, allowing the Parabellum MG14 machine gun to move in a complete circle. He looked around the small space. On one side of the stool was a hole in the floor, into which had been placed the long, boxy lens of a powerful reconnaissance camera the observer employed to take photographs of the land below. A bomb range finder was fixed beside it. On the other side was a *Telefunken* wireless transmitter unit for sending Morse messages to the ground. Alec reached down and extracted a well-traveled valise from under the seat.

The valise was unlatched—Ellenor had retrieved the blanket from it—so he quickly located the tobacco and put a match to his first cigarette since departing the aerodrome. It felt divine, like scripture on a Sunday morning. He jumped off the wing, leaned against the plane, and inspected the cigarette package. He couldn't read a word of it. He exhaled a funnel of smoke. "What does Nil mean?"

"It's the German word for the Nile."

"You mean the river?"

She kept her eyes on the pasture. "I suppose so."

He sat on the ground a few feet away from her, the morning world opening up before them. The only sound was that of the chatting birds. "When we go up again, we'll need to keep you warm."

"I have no coat."

"You can wear mine."

"And what will you wear? I know little about flying, but I have recently learned that it's incredibly cold up there."

True enough. And they'd been at only eight thousand feet, which meant the temperature was about thirty degrees colder than it was at ground level. Hildegard could reach over twice that elevation. No one could survive up there without adequate insulation. "I have an idea," he said.

She looked at him and waited.

"There's a village about a mile from here."

"How do you know?"

"I saw it before we landed. It's east, just down the way there. I've no idea who lives there or if it's any kind of proper place at all, but you need better clothing, and I need a bit of time to ponder our situation and find a solution."

"So...we're going to visit this town and...purchase an overcoat?"

"Perhaps. Have you any money?"

She snorted. "Yes, I always keep fifty *Deutsche*

Marks in my left boot whenever I'm stealing airplanes."

"Oh, is that all? I've got at least three hundred hidden in my shorts."

She acknowledged his retort with a partial smile that didn't reach her eyes. "Sorry. What I should have said is no, I don't have any money. I don't have anything but what I'm wearing. I left it all behind."

A lesser woman might have broken down and cried. Ellenor just ripped blades of grass between her fingers.

"Well…" He got back to his feet, then tried and failed to blow a smoke ring. "I guess there's nothing for it but to keep up our thieving ways and steal a coat."

He held his hand out to her and waited.

Chapter Thirteen

Trudging through the wilderness in a part of Germany she'd never visited, Ellenor decided she would personally—by herself, if necessary—end the Great War. She'd do it like this: One, wash her face and apply fresh cosmetics. Two, drive to Kaiser Wilhelm's imperial palace in Berlin. Three, give him a good American kick in the shin and tell him to stop ruining everything.

And what would old King Willy tell her as he rubbed his lower leg? *I didn't ruin everything, Fräulein. You're quite adept at that yourself.*

She walked beside Alec, two hours after dawn. They crossed a heath of mostly open land, dotted with copses of stout evergreens and the occasional elaborate elm. Nothing here was spoiled. Half a mile back they'd come upon a mostly buried caisson stamped with a fading Iron Cross, but otherwise they had seen no evidence that the Fatherland was at war with enemies on two fronts. They found an array of flat stones that allowed them to cross a stream so clear that every glossy pebble was visible under the water.

We gave you employment and a surrogate family, Wilhelm reminded her.

It was true. Despite the war that the Kaiser had declared from his balcony three years ago, Ellenor had constructed a fine and rewarding life, even while men were shredded not far away at Verdun. The French town of Fleury changed hands sixteen times over the course of the protracted battle, and each time, thousands died either to seize it or hold fast to it. That was the definition of futility. And all the while, Ellenor was making fast friends with Germans like Josef and Dagmar. She ate dinner with them almost every evening. They were her family. They liked to laugh. Now she would likely never see them again.

"Care to share your thoughts?" Alec asked. They'd walked silently for the last several minutes, leaving tracks behind that would be gone by noon.

"Sometimes I find it hard to recall what I was doing before my life here in Europe," she said. "It wasn't so long ago. Is that strange?"

"Hardly. I don't think I even existed before the RFC found me."

"What did you do? Before the war, I mean."

"As little as possible. I studied, but not much. I played cricket, but not well."

"That's what I mean. The details seem very far away now."

We gave you Father, Wilhelm said, *and you stabbed a knife in his heart.*

Ellenor pushed the voice away. It was her own.

Alec walked with his hands in the pockets of his flannel pants. "It's enough to make one wonder what the days will hold after the fighting has stopped."

"Have you thought about what you'll do?"

"Fly on, I imagine."

"Fly to where?"

"Oh, I don't know. They say there's a future for aircraft in delivering the post."

"You'll carry mail in an airplane?"

"Sounds unlikely, doesn't it? I suppose I'll just have to take up beekeeping."

"You'll need a lot more lessons."

"Fortunately, I happen to be on good terms with an expert."

"Are we on good terms?"

"Well…you haven't shot me today."

"I seem to have left my rifle behind with everything else."

"Thank God for small favors."

She permitted herself a smile, though not one she honestly felt. She and Alec took the long way around a tangle of wild privet, and houses became visible down the slope, plainly painted homes and fences of stacked stone. Ellenor realized how the two of them must look, a peaceful couple strolling in the midmorning sun, dressed somewhat strangely and both in need of a bath. They were not so out of place. War had created many misfits and outcasts, and it was not uncommon to see the occasional disheveled, haunted-eyed straggler passing through. They spoke in riddles and seldom stayed for long.

"You'll have to do the talking," Alec said.

"I assumed as much. Do we have a story?"

"We're fleeing the Front. We had a farm. French artillery drove us out. Our lorry broke down last night, and we've been walking ever since."

"And if they ask our names?"

"Make something up."

"And if they ask why you're not speaking?"

He shook his head. "I don't know. Tell them I've been shell-shocked or something."

"That's your best explanation? You don't speak because your brain is addled? We should forget this and turn around. I'll help you start the plane so you can go and find your sister. I'll be fine."

"Liar. Besides, I'm responsible for your being here. It's my duty to see this through."

"So I'm your duty now?"

"Please, I'm trying. I'll work it out eventually—soon. I'll find the answer. In the meantime, we could use a bite to eat, and we'll see about that coat. I'm just going to keep my mouth shut and hope for hospitality."

Ellenor hoped for a lot more than that. She hoped she'd wake up and find this was all a dream. She hoped for a way to return to her little room in the manor house, with its brocade drapes and white damask bunting hanging from the bed posts. None of that was possible anymore, but at least she was wearing a decent pair of boots.

They neared the village, with its slate roofs and moss-covered wells. When the first hay farmer looked up from his work and noticed them approaching, Ellenor waved with an enthusiasm she didn't feel and tried to think of a fabricated name.

****

At that same moment, in a barn that had been converted into a hangar, Gustov Voss scraped dried blood from the back of a truck.

"She brought him here in this?"

"She did," Josef confirmed. "When she called me over, I thought it was to help her unload her hive boxes, but instead…"

"Instead it was a British officer."

"I believe that is correct, sir. I mean, Gustov."

The blade of Gustov's knife, made of Damascus steel, was so well-polished that he saw little fragments of his reflection in it when he observed the flaking circle of blood.

"What other injuries did he receive in the crash?"

"Nothing major, from what I understand. But, uh…that blood wasn't from the crash."

Gustov looked over at him, waiting.

"He was bleeding from the hand because Little Fox shot him."

"Little Fox?"

"I mean Ellenor. That's what I call her."

"She shot the Englander?"

"In the hand, yes."

"And then she brought him back here to field-dress the wound she inflicted?"

"I know it sounds unbelievable, but it's true."

Gustov laughed in spite of himself. "Oh, I'm starting to believe that anything is possible when Ellenor Jantz is involved." He darkened when he recalled that he'd not yet filed his report of the incident. Perhaps he could delay it a bit longer. "I ask you again, just to be sure—you have no idea where they've gone?"

"I'm sorry. I didn't know she was going to leave with him."

"I'm told she left all of her possessions behind."

"And her bees."

"Yes. Her beloved bees." Gustov tapped the tip of the knife against his knuckle as he considered it. "They took the plane eastward, but I assumed the pilot would soon change course and head west, in the direction of the Front. That's where the action is. That's where he would likely go. So my men scoured the sky to the west, not returning until their fuel tanks demanded it. And they saw nothing, heard nothing. This makes me think that the Englander continued east after taking off, which makes little sense. What does he expect to do with a single aircraft in the heart of Germany? At most, he might blow up a locomotive or a bridge...and what does that possibly accomplish that's worth the trouble of recruiting a partner and orchestrating the theft of a plane?"

Josef, obviously well out of his element, only shrugged.

"I am missing some vital piece of intelligence." Indeed, it was as if he were working from a script with several important pages removed. "What am I overlooking?"

"I wish I could help you."

"I'm sure you do," Gustov said distractedly. He walked slowly to the barn's wide doorway and summoned his valet with a wave. They'd assigned to him a young man barely out of rifle training, wide freckles like dew drops on his cheeks. All air officers on both sides of the Front enjoyed the services of such an aide-de-camp. Gustov's was a naïve Franconian named Eldwin.

"Sir!" Eldwin saluted with unnecessary formality.

"Where is Lieutenant Mier?"

"Overseeing the refueling for the day's patrol, sir."

"As soon as he's finished, please ask him to come see me."

"Of course, sir."

"That is all."

Eldwin raced away, nothing but skinny knees and flying elbows, and damn the bureaucrat who conscripted boys like this for a war that would eventually kill them. At the very least, it would transform them with its tentacles and bile.

Gustov lit a Turkish cigarette and waited.

Mier arrived on a motorbike eight minutes later, dismounted, and came to attention with a salute not quite as rigid as Eldwin's had been.

Gustov explained the only plan he'd managed to assemble. It was the best he had. It was predicated on a single, possibly pointless hunch: "The Englander was apparently shot down not far from here. We need to find his crashed plane."

Chapter Fourteen

Ellenor sat at an outdoor table made from the repurposed lumber of an old ox cart. A glazed ceramic pot occupied the table's center, roses spilling out of it like fire. Across from her sat a sixty-year-old hay merchant named Rickert and his wife Magnild, the village seamstress and quilt-maker. Alec sat beside her. They drank beer from steins that Magnild stored in the icebox to keep the metal cool.

"...and we left so quickly that we didn't bother to consider our destination," Ellenor continued, making it up as she went along. She'd never considered herself much of a storyteller, but she'd gotten practice with Father's children, who'd grown bored of their books and looked forward to whatever tales Ellenor created from the shadows on their wall. "I can't tell you how much we appreciate your kindness."

"You're in the country," Rickert said. "We remember our manners in the country. Now, try finding an honest man in the city..."

"Oh, hush," his wife admonished him. "Fine people inhabit the cities, and you know it."

"Yes, fine people who would just as soon fleece you for your last coin as give you the time of day. I've done my time in town. I prefer sky over smoke."

"I concur," Ellenor said, hoping to come across as whatever kind of person that Rickert thought was salt of the earth. "We didn't have much at our home, but all the same, it's a shame to leave it all behind." She realized as she lied to this honest man that she was playing a game. For the first time in her adult life, she was actively deceiving someone, a spy in a foreign land, hoodwinking the locals. The idea was so farfetched that she stuttered a few times while talking of the fake property she and her brother Mika had been forced to flee, with its pretty tiled walk and green shutters.

"And you, Mika?" Rickert asked. "What do you do for work?"

Ellenor put on the longsuffering face she'd been practicing in her mind. "My brother doesn't speak, at least not to those he's just met. Please don't be offended."

Rickert seemed at a loss, unsure of how to process this, but Magnild swooped in with that kind of grace acquired only by women of a certain age. "No need to worry about that, dear," she said. "If he's fond of dumplings and Strauss, he'll find himself at home here."

"You have a gramophone?" Ellenor asked.

Rickert grinned like a rogue. "We may be provincial, but we're not barbarians. We have a lovely Berliner I'd be happy to show you."

"And we'd be happy to see it!"

The next hour went like that, with Ellenor weaving threads of gentle lies across a loom until she wondered if she'd be smothered by them before she was through. Johann Strauss' "The Blue Danube" spun on a hand-cranked gramophone. Inevitably the talk went to what everyone called the Great War, though there was nothing great about it but the size of the egos of the men who'd started it. Rickert and Magnild had two daughters in Göttingen, thankfully well removed from the fighting, but the country's economy was so focused on outputting war materiel that both young women had been forced to take up jobs in a machine shop.

"They spend all day making rivets," Magnild explained. "It can't be very rewarding for them."

"They're safe and they're paid for their labor," Rickert said. "A father cares a lot less for *rewarding*, believe me."

Magnild showed them the small studio she used in her work as a seamstress, and it was then that Ellenor discarded the notion of locating a coat. She'd come here intending to acquire an insulated garment to protect her from the temperatures at high altitudes, but now inspiration moved her in a different direction—one that didn't require her to steal what she needed.

She pointed across the room. "That quilt is incredible."

Magnild smiled. "Oh, that old thing is nothing special. I've done far better work."

"It looks heavy and warm."

"I'm afraid the stitching isn't up to my current standards. I made it years ago. It just sits around and waits for winter, when it can finally serve a purpose."

"May I see it?"

"Of course, dear!"

In Ellenor's arms, the quilt lay like a bag of sand, its weight just the kind that one would need to rest comfortably on a frigid night, come November. Ellenor unfolded it carefully, revealing squares of pale yellow and red, connected by interlocking black checks. The squares were made of variegated fabrics: thick flannel, smooth batik, rough homespun.

"The batting is wool," Magnild said. "It's not pretty, but it's warm."

"Would you consider trading for it?"

"Trading?"

Ellenor folded the bulky blanket and put it aside. Then she reached into the rolled neck of her sweater and revealed the honey bee pendant that Father had given her. She unclasped it. The thought of parting with it made her sad, as it was the one real piece of jewelry that she owned. "It's made of pewter and feldspar," she explained. "Those aren't rare materials, but neither are they commonplace. This should be worth a bit if you choose to sell it." She held it out.

Alec and Rickert looked on as Magnild accepted the necklace. The metal flashed in her palm. "If you need the quilt, dear, just take it. You shouldn't give away your last possession."

"I insist. It's only fair."

"You won't accept a gift?"

"I won't. You've been very gracious. And these days, that's hard to find. We're all so worried that the world is ending that we forget who we are. You've not forgotten."

"And neither have you, apparently."

"Well…that remains to be seen."

Rickert slowly raised his hand, like a schoolboy waiting his turn. "May I ask a question, lass?"

"Of course."

"I'm very thankful for the bauble there. I'm sure it will come in handy at the market. But, um…might I ask why you'd be needing a blanket like that in the middle of summer?"

It was a reasonable question, and one that Ellenor hadn't prepared herself to answer. So instead of staining her already soiled soul with another inaccuracy, she defaulted to the truth. "As hard as it is for me to believe, I'm about to take a trip, a journey to somewhere I've never been before. Quite honestly, I'm a little bit afraid. I've left everything meaningful behind, and all I can do is hope that I'll be all right. It's happening so suddenly that I've not yet had time to sit and cry about it. I'm sure I'll get to that. But until then, I just want to stay warm."

Rickert seemed satisfied by this. He might have still been curious about the need for a heavy cover, as summer temperatures were such that you could sleep comfortably at night with only a single cotton sheet, but he was savvy enough to keep his mouth shut. Something wasn't right with these two; they tried to hide it, but it was there, like an animal growling just beyond the limit of your campfire light.

"Where are the two of you headed from here?" Magnild wondered.

"East, I think."

"Away from the violence, then."

"I hope so." For some reason, she doubted that were true.

****

Alec walked toward the setting sun, carrying a bartered quilt under one arm and a sack of food under the other.

By dusk they'd made their way back to where Hildegard, their lady-in-waiting, rested patiently in the low pasture grass. Alec admired her as they approached. Her blunt nose was upswept, as if seeking the sky. She was painted in an alternating three-color scheme of gray, green, and rusty brown. Her struts and wheel covers were a pale, unblemished blue. If not for the black crosses outlined in white, she would have been beautiful. But it was that cross that would permit Alec to fly freely in German skies. It was his passport to an unmolested landing on the outskirts of Metz.

Or so he hoped.

When he'd originally departed the aerodrome in the Avro, which was clearly marked with British cockades, he'd intended to fly at maximum altitude to avoid all conflict and set down at night a good distance from Metz. Then he'd conceal the plane in the brush and head into the city on foot, counting on luck. Now, thanks to Hildegard, he could soar with impunity.

He carefully settled his load in the plane's shadow and stretched. Then he walked around the wings and inspected her. Everything was pristine. A Hebel flare gun was clipped within reach of the observer's seat, along with multicolored flares for signaling ground forces and artillery crews. A hooded compass was mounted into the lower right wing, visible from the cockpit. All the wires were tight. He finished his circuit, his admiration deepening for the Rumpler. "With bellies full of good German meat," he said, "we shall settle down and watch the stars appear. Sounds grand, eh?"

Ellenor had slung off the burlap bag of supplies they'd given her and was rubbing her neck. "We were fortunate to have found the right people."

"Fortune had nothing to do with it, old girl. Haven't you heard? God is on the side of the Allies."

"I'm not much of a churchgoer, but I think God is on the side of not killing each other."

"The way I see it"—he plopped down on the ground and grabbed the canteen—"the Germans and Italians think they've got God in their trenches, and the French think *they're* the chosen ones—"

"And the British?"

"Well, we're just here for the Cognac." He tipped the canteen at her, eliciting a smile. "My point is that God can't be on everyone's side, because someone has to be good and someone else has to be evil. We've just not yet sorted out which one is which. It's troubling, really."

"You don't seem particularly troubled."

"I am a flyer. My stick and my flask comfort me, and I shall not want."

"Are all airmen so flippant? Bombers will soon be on their way to demolish part of the city that we're visiting tomorrow, and you're making light of God and talking about drinking."

"It's either that or go mad." He wiped his mouth on his sleeve. "Do you know that one-third of all British pilots who've died since 1914 have been killed while training? It's true. They never saw the enemy at all. Their crates broke apart. Or they landed poorly. Or they veered the bloody thing into a walnut tree. Every time I go up, I cheat the devil by coming down safely again. Jesting about it all is the way to avoid the asylum." A thought occurred to him, and he leaned toward her. "Do you want to hear a rhyme?"

"A rhyme?"

He didn't wait for an invitation: "The flyer he lay bleeding and in minutes he'd be dead. We listened to his fading words and this is what he said: 'Take the cylinder out of my kidney and the connecting rod out of my brain. From my arse remove the crankshaft and assemble the bloody damn engine again!'"

Ellenor laughed, which pleased Alec, and he considered rolling out a second, equally ribald verse, when she said, "How will you get all three of us to France if there are only two seats in this plane?"

Alec bit his lip. So much for harmless banter. He'd been turning the conundrum over in his mind during the walk back from Rickert's cottage. Three people, two seats. No other way across the border. Germany's entire western edge was a fishnet of razor wire, shell holes, sniper zones, and marshes floating with bodies. Every square mile of ground along the Hindenburg Line was either watched by machine-gun nests or already pounded into broken rock. The water was polluted with chemical runoff from nerve agents and leaking corpses. The forests were blackened stumps. The opposite border led to Russia. That left only the north, where the North Sea might provide a willing ship to England, but Metz was over three hundred miles from the shore.

"I knew there wasn't a way," Ellenor said, reading his thoughts.

"Bugger that. There's always a way."

"Is that a military motto?"

"It's *my* motto, goddammit." He screwed the cap onto the canteen and got to his feet. The sun melted into the horizon; stars opened their eyes. "Tomorrow morning we'll climb into Hildegard here. You'll wrap yourself in your new blanket. We'll get to Metz and find Sarah. Then the three of us, together, we'll figure this out."

"And if we don't?"

"Then we'll leave the city, wait for the bombs to fall, and then reassess the situation. Perhaps Sarah will know of some safe place to go. Perhaps she has friends who can help. I don't know. I haven't received a letter from her in…in a long time." That was the worst part, not knowing if his twin and best friend was getting along all right when all the rest of the world was crumbling. "But we'll figure it out."

That seemed to satisfy her. Then again, she was an accomplished actress, as evidenced by her performance for Rickert and Magnild, so odds were that she was hiding a whole horse cart full of fear, anger, and regret. Alec was not the first man to be vexed by a woman's unspoken thoughts.

"We leave at dawn?" she asked after a while.

"At first light, yes. Thanks to our new friends, we'll have a fine breakfast."

"Where are we sleeping tonight?"

"Mother Earth, I suppose." He'd make a pillow of his flight jacket. He wondered about finding petrol to refuel in Metz. "It's a warm night. Sleeping under a sky free of artillery bursts will be a welcome change."

"The last time I slept outside was in New Mexico."

"Where's that?"

"Just around the corner."

"I thought as much. Nice place?"

"If you like deserts and no government telling you what to do."

"Sounds splendid. I'll holiday there the first chance I get."

"Alec?"

He could barely see her in the dark. "Hmmm?"

"Would you sit beside me?"

He hung there for a moment, then two, unsure of himself in a way he hadn't been since spiraling downward in the Avro, anticipating the impact. Her request was simple. He had asked her to tug down on a propeller, and now—twelve hours later—she was asking him to take a seat next to her.

Silently he went to her in the dark and sat down, cross-legged. Ellenor's knees were near her chest, her arms wrapped around them. Alec could chat endlessly in a mess hall full of men, and he could sing with natural musical ability whenever he was asked to accompany the piano player in a pub on Rue Whatever-The-Hell while carousing in Paris. But now he searched around for words, perhaps something to make her laugh again, and he found only a vacancy where all the proper apologies and proverbs should have been.

They shared that space without speaking, the plane with its guns and bombs only a few feet behind them, biding its time. If Alec expected Ellenor to criticize his lack of a plan or to quietly question what tomorrow would bring, she surprised him by letting the sky darken and the starlight form patterns overhead. The answers might be up there somewhere, so together they stared upward, searching.

Chapter Fifteen

The dog licked Gustov across the mouth. He awoke instantly, grimacing as he rolled away from the sour mutt and sat up. He wiped his lips on his nightshirt, scowling in the dark. Dawn had not yet arrived. What time was it? It felt like the middle of the night, but his instincts told him that sunrise wasn't far away.

The dog nuzzled his leg.

"All right, you savage, come here." He found the dog's head in the gloom and scratched him vigorously, then yawned through a much-needed stretch. This room they'd given him was charming, but the mattress had seen its better day. As for the dog, it had ridden here in Schmit's Fokker, curled up on the man's lap, the squadron mascot who went by the somewhat irreverent name of Pope Benedict.

"That's enough, Pope." Gustov eased him away and stood up, enjoying the sensation of every muscle as it came back to life. His borrowed room was on the second floor of the manse. He threw open the shutters and filled his lungs with the air of a new morning.

Yesterday they'd spotted the Englander's downed plane from the air.

Duty had intervened, however, before they could examine the debris. In response to the United States' entry into the fray a few months ago, the Air Service had mandated an immediate increase in plane production and manpower. While overburdened factories churned out additional engines and untested recruits were pressed into combat duty, new squadrons were formed to ensure air supremacy. The Air Service referred to this heightened output as the *Amerikaprogram*, and it meant that Gustov had little time for personal quests. He and his men had spent yesterday on patrol, flying a defensive line that ran parallel to the Front. Their efforts amounted to nothing more than wasted fuel, as they met only a pair of British DH.4s that immediately turned tail and vanished into a snarl of rain clouds. The only good thing to come of it was that all his boys returned safely to their new airfield and spent the evening getting sauced. Gustov recorded as much in his daily logs.

Today, then, he would personally visit the remains of the wrecked craft.

The house cook, a ruddy-faced woman named Dagmar, prepared a breakfast of cold meat slices, soft-boiled eggs, and warm sourdough bread smeared with honey that Gustov assumed was made possible by Ellenor Jantz. He'd never met a beekeeper, male or female. He wondered if all beekeepers were part of some secret cabal of wartime mischief-makers. They supplied spread for your toast and sold stolen airplane parts to underworld dealers.

Gustov smiled at himself, thanked Dagmar for the meal, and went outside just in time to see a ribbon of pink unfurl itself on the eastern horizon. Pope trotted by, already in pursuit of the scent of rabbits that had come to nibble the grass. Gustov located a motorbike in the barn where supplies they'd brought with them were stored.

The vehicle was little more than a bicycle with an engine attached. Gustov's squadron had been given a pair of NSU 1913 models, named after the city in which they were manufactured, Neckarsulm. All things being equal, Gustov would have preferred a horse. But the stable master, Josef, was evidently still in bed, and Gustov wouldn't have dreamed of waking him up for such a petty request.

He mounted the bike and pulled his aviator goggles over his eyes.

The ride up the hill proved invigorating. The sun rose higher. The air smelled sweet. He slowed as he made his way along the ragged track, careful not to put the bike's front tire into one of the cracks in the hardened mud. If he broke his neck on the back of this shuddering thing, his men would never let him hear the end of it. The finest pilot next to Richthofen, crunched by his own wheel spokes.

Had the squadron not spotted the wreckage from the air, Gustov never would have located it. The wood and canvas were hidden well off the path, flattened in vines of yellow flowers. He killed the NSU's engine and dismounted, removing his goggles and trudging toward a tail fin barely visible above the weeds.

He came upon the burned bus, put his hands on his hips, and observed.

Both wing decks had sheared away upon striking the earth; the lower one was folded back and forth upon itself like a musician's concertina, while the upper was snapped in half and lying ten meters away. One aileron was missing. The green canvas had been shredded when momentum dragged the two-seater across the ground. The barrel of the Lewis gun mounted at the observer's seat was bent like a crooked finger.

Gustov crouched. No explosives were clamped to the plane's undercarriage.

He stood back up. Interesting. The craft had not been on a bombing run, then, so its mission must have been observation—yet the Englander was alone when he arrived wounded at the barn, with no second crewman who operated a camera. Had the observer been killed?

Gustov stepped through the ruined struts and peered into the gunner's seat. There was no sign of blood. Bullet holes dotted the fuselage and had ruptured the fuel tank, igniting a small fire, but there was no evidence that any rounds had struck the two seats.

"The Englander had no payload and no observer." He said this out loud, hoping it would make more sense when he heard himself utter it.

No detonations had been reported on the ground that day—Gustov has confirmed as much with telegraphed reports from local posts—which meant two things, neither of which made sense: *This plane left France carrying no bombs and no observation capabilities.* The only other reason to be in the sky was to shoot down enemy combatants, but you certainly didn't choose a lumbering craft like this when you went hunting single-seat fighters as maneuverable as mosquitoes.

And somewhere in the middle of this puzzle was Ellenor Jantz.

Gustov had always favored action over contemplation. So he discarded his questions and continued his search. He pulled himself toward the pilot's seat, which sat at an odd angle, as the entire machine leaned awkwardly on its side.

He saw the map immediately.

Clipped to a wire near the magneto was a waxed map with something written across the bottom. Gustov pulled it free, stepped away from the plane's shadow, and observed the document in the fresh morning light.

The map depicted much of the Imperial Territory known as Alsace-Lorraine, the multicultural borderland that Germany had annexed after swatting the French in 1871. Gustov stood in Lorraine at this very moment; the land around him was being torn apart by lions on both sides, its citizens half German, half French, a dysfunctional mix of loyalties, architectures, religions, and business pursuits.

Along the map's lower edge, someone had printed two words: AVENUE FOCH.

The word *avenue* wasn't German, but it was used often enough in towns across Europe that Gustov knew he was looking at a street name. But a street in which city? At least two dozen appeared on the map. Gustov wasn't particularly familiar with any of them. But he was certain of this: one of the places on this map was the destination of Ellenor and the Englander she'd aided. In fact, they'd probably already arrived.

But what were they *doing* there? And how could he stop them before they were gone?

He turned and—map in hand—ran back to the motorbike.

****

The time had come again to fly.

Ellenor tried to work the cramp from her neck. She'd slept atop Magnild's quilt, and her rest had been surprisingly complete. The nighttime sounds had woken her once or twice, but both times she'd stared up at the endless sky for only a few minutes before being hypnotized back into sleep. For want of an adequate pillow, though, she'd developed a kink.

"Refreshed and ready to go?" she heard Alec say.

"Neither."

"How about bread and jam, then?"

"And hot tea?"

"Would you settle for canteen water?"

Ellenor spread her arms wide, like wings of her own, aware that the air on summer mornings was somehow both warm and cool. And then she realized something far more important: she was going to have to use the toilet where there was no toilet.

She looked around. It wouldn't be her first time squatting in the wilderness, but you could get away with such things when you were a girl tromping through the sagebrush behind your childhood home. "Thank you for breakfast. I'll join you in a few minutes."

"Right-o." He seemed to understand her unspoken explanation without being told, and he won points for not saying *What are you talking about?* and embarrassing her. She watched him work for a moment, humming as he assembled their meal, and then she walked off until she found a semi-private spot.

When she returned, she discovered that he'd conscripted her quilt into service as a picnic cloth. Arrayed before her was the food supplied by Rickert and Magnild, most of which they had produced themselves, with the exception of the crackers purchased with ration coupons. Ellenor took a seat and concentrated on appreciating the taste of the wild blueberry jam instead of letting herself think about all the ways the coming day could go wrong. But there was no helping it. "Today we go to Metz?" she asked, knowing the answer.

"If I can find it."

"Are we lost?"

"I have the map mostly committed to memory, though my planned route didn't include an interlude in your bee shed and a flight of several hours in the dark. But if I can make out a landmark or two once we reach altitude, we'll be fine. Actually, I'm rather inept when it comes to most things in life, but I can sing and navigate and handle a plane with the best of them. That's about it."

"You sing?"

"I am renowned in French pubs for just such an ability."

"So...you sing drinking songs."

"Let's call it an occupational hazard."

"You're confident you can find the city just by...looking around?"

"As easily as I can find a Parisian cabaret."

"You're awfully glib for someone doing what you're doing, stealing a plane and trying to outrace a bombing raid."

"Some days, it's either be glib or go mad. Other men favor gallows humor, but that's always seemed too cynical for me." He chewed, swallowed, licked his lips. "You say anything to distract yourself, really, from the thought of what could happen to you on any given afternoon. I'd rather be flippant than fatalistic any day."

"Such is the life of a Tommy, I suppose. That's what they call you, isn't it? A British soldier is a

Tommy?"

"The poor bloody infantry are the Tommies. They're the sassy lads facing poison gas and trench foot on a daily basis. They're the ones who will win or lose this vile scrap for us. Me…" He shrugged. "I'm just an acrobat with flimsy wooden wings strapped to his back. We flyers are fighting a type of dream war. I don't think it really counts."

"It counts for your mother back home. It counts for those who care about you and want to see you survive."

"I assume so. I used to write letters to my mum every week. But it started to feel as if I were writing about someone else's life. What about you?"

"What about me?"

"Do you write home?"

"Not as often as I should."

"What would you tell them about what you're doing now?"

She had no real answer for that. What she was doing now was inventing herself anew with every decision she made. She was already a plane thief and a quilt trader. What would she become today? "How big is your sister?"

He frowned. "What do you mean?"

"Could Sarah and I both fit into that second seat?"

Alec glanced up at the plane he called Hildegard. "I suppose if we unbolted the seat itself, two people could cram themselves in there, but it would be dreadfully uncomfortable, and you couldn't maintain it for very long."

"For long enough?"

He made a doubting face.

"If we had no other choice?" she asked.

"I simply don't know. Either way, we'd need to remove some of the munitions in the egg basket to account for the added weight." He stood up. "Now, the French squadron arrives in the skies over Metz in two days. So as much as I honestly enjoy sitting here with you, and I really do, I'm afraid it's time to shove off."

She was enjoying it, as well, in a way that surprised her. Take away the war, and you had the perfect morning—minus the part about relieving herself in the weeds—and she hated to put away their meager things and move on. She liked the way he grinned when making a joke.

"What's wrong?" he asked.

"I'm not about to tell you."

"You don't trust me? I don't see why not. It's not like I've ruined your life or anything."

She almost smiled, but instead only nodded and gathered up the blanket. A few minutes later, she was back at her post in front of the propeller—or airscrew, as Alec sometimes called it—waiting for the word: *Contact*.

Alec settled in behind the control wheel, though he'd told her that most planes used a *joystick*—the least subtle bit of innuendo that Ellenor had ever heard. He pulled on his cap and donned his goggles and the beekeeping gloves she'd given him.

He gave the word.

The engine fired on the second attempt. Ellenor raced around the wing and scrambled up the fuselage. She lowered herself into position, then cocooned herself in the quilt.

The plane rolled forward.

Ellenor waited for the rush of wind and nerves, and

the rush came. It made her bones heavy at first as her back was pressed against the seat and her tailbone was shaken by the bumps in the field. But then it changed from heavy to light as the wheels left the earth, and then light became no weight at all.

She peeked from her shell and watched the green world fall away. It was beautiful and frightening and serene.

She couldn't help it: she laughed aloud.

Chapter Sixteen

Protected by his Iron Crosses, Alec Corbin-Dawes of Derbyshire flew deeper into *Deutschland.* His disguise permitted him to soar as low as five thousand feet, offering a vivid view of the landscape below. At this elevation on a summer day, the air was as warm as English beer.

Referring to Hildegard's compass, he kept a northeasterly bearing. Metz was conveniently placed at the confluence of the Seille River and the Moselle, so as soon as he spotted either one of them, he could locate the city. With his bloodstained blue scarf protecting his neck from chafing against his collar, he turned his head frequently left and right, doing double duty as both pilot and observer. Vineyards lay below, little terraced rectangles of wine country. Ruined stonework forts from a previous age had been converted into barns.

Whenever he twisted in his seat to check on Ellenor, he found her staring this way and that, excited by everything she saw below. He'd been the same on his first few flights, eyes agape, heart somewhere in the back of his throat. Mankind was not meant to fly, so doing it was an act of defiance. It felt that way.

He turned back around just in time to see the planes approaching.

Shit.

They came in the standard *Kette* or chain formation

that all Germans pilots favored, with one leader and a wingman followed by other pairs in a linked echelon. There were eight of them.

Alec rolled his tongue against his lower lip. Ellenor grabbed his shoulder, and he nodded. *Yes, of course I see them, old girl.*

Their noses were painted blue, their wing decks a desert tan. They were a mix of Albatros fighters, most of them the sprightly D.III models. With two guns each, they were capable of bringing sixteen barrels right at him. They were two hundred yards away and closing.

Alec tightened his hands on the control wheel.

Hold steady, for Christ's sake.

But that was far easier said than done. He'd faced large numbers of the enemy before, but he was usually accompanied by several of his own birds, evening the odds. On his best day, he'd taken out two of the enemy and winged a third, but he'd been in The Dragon that afternoon and full of grit and guile. Today he was none of those things.

Their howling propellers looked like black circles as they neared.

Were they going to fire on him? Alec snapped from his trance and checked his gun. In addition to the swivel-mounted weapon at the observer's seat, Hildegard sported a fixed-position 7.92-millimeter light machine gun, synchronized with the propeller so that it could spit out its bullets without shooting off the spinning blades. Alec prepared to fire by engaging the cocking lever. He flexed his fingers. If the Huns decided to attack, he wouldn't be able to take them all out, but if he cleared two in the center of the formation, he might be able to get Hildegard down near the ground so they could at least land safely before they were blown to splinters.

The lead Albatros was almost directly in front of him, just off to his left side. The others held a practiced formation behind their leader. Alec took a breath and waited for their response.

The German planes passed within thirty yards of him and kept going. One of the pilots waved.

Alec, dumbfounded, lifted a hand.

Then they were gone.

Too stunned even to turn and watch them go, Alec released his death grip on the trigger.

Behind him, Ellenor said something that sounded like a relieved curse. All Alec could manage was a weak thumbs-up.

The sky offered no further threats. Down below, the land looked like the cover of a charming children's book, with everything divided up into fastidious little squares. Nothing indicated how close they'd almost come to the enemy's teeth.

Alec smiled broadly, stupidly, swallowing the warm air.

By and by he returned to the matter at hand. The luck of a gambler could run dry at any particular moment, so he focused on his gauges, noting the petrol supply and doing a quick bit of math. All was well—for now.

Twenty minutes later, they came upon the river.

Alec aligned Hildegard with the course of the Moselle. The silver-blue water looked idyllic from here, winding through farms and little villages and carefully sculpted fields where they grew Riesling and other grapes. The region had belonged to France until about fifty years ago, and now the Germans understood the joys of a good pinot noir. No wonder the French wanted it back.

They flew for miles like that. Alec had forgotten what it was like, being airborne and not worrying about getting jumped by Fritz. Flying was pure. You owed no one anything up here, not even gravity, and no one owed you. For millennia men had dreamed of doing the very thing that Alec and Ellenor were doing right now. Inventors had constructed pipe frames and flaps; naturalists had drawn countless bird wings; fools had jumped.

"And here we are."

He wished he could turn around in his seat and share the moment with her, as he suspected she was experiencing similar feelings. But then chimney smoke appeared on the horizon.

The first thing he saw of Metz was its balloon.

German observation balloons, known as *Drachen* to the natives, were hundred-foot horizontal brown bags of hydrogen that allowed an observer in a dangling basket to see great distances. The British, with their usual impudence, called them sausages.

Ellenor leaned forward and yelled: "What is that?"

"A lookout!"

The massive balloon floated over a thousand feet up and was tethered to the ground by a mooring cable. Usually such things were positioned just behind the Front as a way of targeting artillery bombardments; the man in the basket used a wireless radio device, signal flares, or even colored streamers to inform the gun crews how to pinpoint their attack. A man at one thousand feet with the proper optics could, on a clear day, see forty miles in every direction. Other balloons were kitted out with photographic cameras so that pictures could be produced of enemy emplacements.

This one was a watchdog. No doubt the observer in his wicker roost had used his field glasses and watched Hildegard approach. His task was to alert anti-aircraft personnel about incoming threats. If the bombing raid were to be successful here, the French scout planes would need to drop down unnoticed from the clouds and use incendiary rounds to light the sausage on fire before the big steel-framed Breguet bombers arrived to raze the factory. And by then, Sarah needed to be far away.

Alec gave the balloon a wide berth and continued on to Metz.

The city soon sprawled beneath him, but he didn't waste time ogling it. More than sixty thousand people lived here, and the longer he and Ellenor remained aloft, the more eyes that would find them, and that meant more curiosity, more questions. He lowered the plane's nose and reduced speed as he swept out and around the edge of the urban center. He looked for a suitable place to put down and located one about two miles from the city, tucked behind a hill. The field was blocked on three sides by trees, which was good, and there was no farmhouse nearby, which was also good. Alec didn't have quite as much surface area as he would have liked, but he'd landed planes on plots of land the size of an envelope before, so he brazenly cut the engine and let Hildegard glide silently to earth.

****

Ellenor, feet again on *terra firma*, suddenly recalled the Yiddish word that Josef had taught her:

bashert. She had never believed in a preordained life. You crossed the bridges you built yourself, not ones that some team of celestial carpenters had constructed on your behalf.

She and Alec spent nearly an hour concealing the plane with deadfall, weeds, and slender limbs broken from walnut trees. It was not a perfect disguise, but Alec surmised that it would be sufficient to fool the casual observer.

"Shall we, then?" he asked, stowing his insulated coat in the plane.

Ellenor pushed up her sweater sleeves. "To the factory?"

"Straight to Sarah's house, actually. She lives on a street called Foch—at least she did the last time we exchanged correspondence. I always addressed the post to Sarah Weller of Foch Street. Still sounds peculiar, her having a different last name." He pointed. "At any rate, we should get moving."

Ellenor felt like there was more to say. The flight had been exhilarating. She wanted to talk about it, to ask him if it was always that way, to bring back the grin that had only now faded from her face. Flying was just as children believed it to be when they lay on their backs in the grass and imagined swinging on vines between the clouds.

Alec set off for the city, and she matched his strides.

After a few minutes, she said, "How long did it take you to learn?"

"To learn what?"

"How to operate an airplane."

"A few weeks, I suppose."

"That's all?"

"Well, the RFC is always in something of a rush to get boys into the air, but yes, it's just a matter of listening to lectures and then sitting in a wingless tub to practice the stick and rudder bar. When it's finally time to get into the air, every man starts as an observer, just to see if you're going to vomit the first time you leave the ground. I didn't, by the by."

"What about women?"

"What about them?"

"Are there any female pilots?"

"Good Lord, I should think not."

"What's that supposed to mean?"

"How many women do you know who drive automobiles? I can count them on one hand."

"If it weren't for my driving an automobile, you'd still be lying on a hillside."

"I'm not saying you *shouldn't* drive. It's just uncommon that you *do*."

"I've been doing a lot of uncommon things lately."

"That makes two of us. I'm absent without leave. As far as anyone knows at the aerodrome, I embarked on an unauthorized solo patrol flight and never returned."

"And if you make it back there? If you get your sister safely to the other side, how will you account for yourself?"

"I'll face a court-martial, presumably."

"They'll arrest you?"

"Undoubtedly." He smiled at her, ever game for a challenge. "My new plan is to blame everything entirely on you."

"I believe, sir, the evidence does not support your

claim."

"Never let the lack of hard evidence prevent you from shifting all blame to someone else. Shakespeare said that, you know."

"He did, huh?"

"Well, I paraphrased him, of course. He had a few more *thous* and *shalts* in there."

She rolled her eyes but favored him with a smile of her own. "I'm sure he did."

They walked in silence, watching the city grow larger. A place of industry and commerce, Metz pushed smoke into the sky from hundreds of flues. Ellenor became very aware of how she was dressed. No one in the city would approve. Even a woman performing wartime work was rarely seen in trousers, unless she was tromping behind a plow. Uniforms were perfectly acceptable, but the top was always paired with a calf-length dress. If not engaged in some type of labor in support of the war effort, ladies across Europe wore the *Kriegskrinoline*, a suit-and-skirt combination that might have been more practical than previous fashions, without all those cumbersome hoops, but it was certainly no good for keeping out angry bees during a hive inspection. Ellenor hoped her unusual attire wouldn't rouse too much suspicion.

"Are you worried about how it will be when you see your sister again?" she asked.

"What do you mean by 'how it will be'?"

"You know, are you nervous? You've not seen her in a long time."

"That's true, and I am. The war shut everything down. It's like the world went dark. The letters simply stopped coming. I want to make sure she's all right."

Ellenor heard the raw concern in his voice. She was an only child and couldn't feel whatever it was he was feeling, but she shared his sense of loss. Ellenor was now homeless. If she spent too much time thinking about that, she'd have a breakdown right here on the side of the well-rutted road, *bashert* be damned.

They reached the outskirts of Metz by midmorning. Keeping away from the main road into the city, they walked among the simple homes of vineyard workers, farmers, and shepherds. They saw only the young and the old; everyone in the middle was either off fighting somewhere or providing a support function in a factory or on the back of a truck. Military service for fit young men was compulsory, so jobs were reassigned. Ellenor and Alec passed a woman delivering milk, a boy of no more than thirteen changing a truck tire, and a pair of white-haired men repairing a levee. Alec was the exception, so he kept his head down and his back hunched, his hands buried in his pockets.

"Where is this Foch Street?" Ellenor asked without looking at him.

"No idea. Luckily I have a fluent partner."

"Partner? What was your original plan? How did you intend to find your sister before almost crashing into my bees?"

"I have a little German. Not much. But I can manage to ask for directions. And to find the local pub."

She shook her head. "You're nearly impossible."

"I appreciate the 'nearly.' There's someone there. She looks harmless enough."

By now they'd entered the city proper, the street made of bricks, the rooftops of gray slate. A woman in a gingham dress swept the dirt from the porch of what appeared to be a cobbler's shop, with shoes of practical designs on display in one narrow window. No one bought anything. These days, folks wore their shoes until the soles crumbled, spending their small earnings on food, medicine, and tobacco. Everything else could wait.

Ellenor approached the woman, said hello, and asked about the Wellers of Foch Street.

"Not familiar with any Wellers," the woman said. She leaned heavily on her broom, her face red and hard. She was the right age to have sons at war. If they'd been sent west, they were likely pinned down in Belgium somewhere. If they'd gone east, they were fighting the Russians, who'd been in general disarray since the revolution in February but were still quite adept at killing hotheaded Germans. The cobbler-woman's eyes said as much.

"Can you tell me how to find the street?" Ellenor asked.

The woman provided simple directions and returned immediately to her work, as if sensing the danger of speaking too long to a stranger.

Ellenor rejoined Alec. "This way."

"What did she say?"

"Very little."

"She knew of the street?"

"Yes, but not of any Mr. and Mrs. Weller. If we find them, it's *bashert*, and if not, that's *bashert,* too."

"I'm not familiar with that word."

"It's like…destiny."

"Ah. A good destiny, I hope."

"Not necessarily. That's the point."

The city proper rose up around them, the avenues becoming cramped, twisting things with no logic behind their layout. On either side of these streets stood buildings of yellow limestone that ran abruptly into the modern and very Germanic architecture of the town's more recent rulers. A fishmonger in the brightest apron Ellenor had ever seen hailed them from a corner stall, motioning to the catch his young sons had pulled from the Moselle just the night before. Ellenor waved a *no, thank you* and crossed the street in the wake of a rattletrap truck spewing blue fumes.

"Again," she said, "I wonder how you'd planned on finding anyone in this city on your own in the dark."

"I've always gotten lucky. I'd planned on starting at a tavern."

"And trade drinking songs for directions?"

"You don't approve of drinking with the enemy?"

"They're not the enemy."

"Well...*somebody* is."

A pair of mules was hitched to a wagon in front of an ice house. Boys loaded canvas-wrapped blocks into the wagon and packed them with straw. A woman sold faded flowers from a cart, while gossips in head scarves stood on the corner and caught up on the daily roster of rumors. The people conducted their business with occasional glances at the sky; German airships had been bombing London, so surely repercussions were to follow. Their talk was a mixture not only of languages but of dialects within those languages. Old women who'd been born French seventy years ago had become Germans when their city changed hands, and now they were something uniquely in between: Messines, a people who had learned to bargain, to complain mostly in secret, and to survive.

"What is your brother-in-law's name?" Ellenor asked, eyeing an elderly couple holding hands beneath an unlit gaslight. They held bags of potatoes.

"I'm sorry?"

"Sarah's husband. What's his name?"

"Uh, Stefan. Stefan Weller. But we're not looking for him. He's dead, remember? Sarah is a widow. They were married for only two years before he passed."

"I thought the property might still be under his name, or that someone might remember him. Stay here." Ellenor crossed the street and steeled herself to again pretend to be someone she was not. She fastened a smile to her face, said good morning, and inquired about the Wellers, and when they told her that an *Herr* Weller resided near the old granary just up the street, she thanked them and wondered randomly what Father had told Karl and Truda about her sudden disappearance. Did they now believe she'd deceived them? Had all the fondness they felt for her been replaced by something else?

"Well?" Alec asked when she returned to him.

"A man named Weller lives not far from here."

"A man? So...a relative of Stefan's, perhaps?"

"We'll see. This way."

She wanted to wash her clothes. And after they were clean, she wanted to write a letter to Father and try to explain. He probably thought her a monster. And she still wanted to know why half of her bees had died.

They followed a wide, cobbled street, sand-colored buildings wedged closely together on either side, their balconies festooned with mementoes for those at the Front. Half-feral dogs were everywhere. On the corner stood a statue of some colonial hero from the Wahehe War in Africa. A warehouse-like building that looked as old as the Roman Empire served as a granary. Directly across the street from it was a two-story home with shutters closed on all the windows but one. Above the house's wooden doorframe was a pair of interlocked cherubs, their coating of gold leaf mostly gone. One of the angels was missing an arm. A metal plaque bore the family name in Gothic lettering: WELLER.

"This may not be the right place," she reminded him.

"I suppose we'll know soon enough."

They approached the door, guarded by its faded angels. Alec let out a long breath. Ellenor had the sudden impulse to give his hand an encouraging squeeze, but she thought better of it. Then she said to hell with that and did it anyway.

He gave her a strained smile in return, then drummed the butt of his fist on the door.

Chapter Seventeen

Gustov lost a pilot that morning.

Eleven Fokker triplanes had taken to the sky shortly after dawn, charged with delivering support to an armored column that was falling back to a more strategic position about ten kilometers from No Man's Land. The troops had taken a pounding from a pair of French 75-millimeter field guns and needed to regroup and tend to the wounded. Gustov's squadron covered the soldiers from the air, but they ran afoul of a swarm of Spads an hour into their mission.

One of the newer men, Kasper, a clarinet player from Hanover, had gotten his elevator shredded when a pair of the Frog bastards had fallen on him from behind. His crate rolled over at two thousand meters, its wheels pointed straight up, and Kasper fell from the cockpit. Gustov, arriving seconds too late, watched the poor man drop, arms and legs batting madly. Gustov's own molten rage startled him, and he screamed the entire time he was emptying his guns into Kasper's killers.

Ten planes landed behind Father's barn. The mechanics and valets rushed out, already knowing that their family had lost one of its own. They would eulogize him tonight with liquor and somber tunes played on the parlor's grand piano.

Now, just after the noon hour, Gustov left them to their subdued talk in the marble-lined dining hall and the meal that dear Dagmar had prepared. He had no appetite. His valet, Eldwin, waited for him outside the door.

The young man stiffened to full attention and kept his eyes straight ahead. "Sir."

"The papers?"

Eldwin handed him a bundle of communiques. Gustov leafed through them. He'd ordered Eldwin to send word of the Englander to all nearby posts. Yet for all the advances in wireless radio, the German war machine still received most of its messages in the diplomatic pouches of men on motorbikes. Thus it would take days for word of the stolen Rumpler to be disseminated to every city on the Englander's map. Gustov had no intention of waiting that long.

"Have the mechanics refueled my bird?"

"They have, sir. All is shipshape."

"Good. Thank you." He handed the papers back to the younger man and asked himself why he hadn't mentioned Miss Jantz in his otherwise highly detailed report to High Command. He had no answer for that.

"What next, sir?"

"You confirmed that Avenue Foch is located in Metz?"

"Yes, sir. Several of the men have spent their leave in Metz and are familiar with the town. I confirmed their statements an hour ago with our people in the city itself."

"Your efficiency never ceases to amaze me. You honor your family name."

"Thank you, sir. Sincerely."

Gustov, suddenly emotional, gripped the younger man's shoulder. "Take the rest of the day off. Get something to eat. Join the others tonight to bid our brother Kasper goodbye."

"I will, sir. Good hunting."

From there, Gustov went to his room, where Eldwin had laid out a fresh set of flying garb, having taken this morning's outfit to the washerwoman for cleaning. He stripped off his field tunic with its precise markings of rank and donned the unadorned, more liberating attire of a flyer: heavy corduroy trousers lined with fleece, a field-gray sweater, and a double-breasted long coat with a wide lambs-wool collar that could be turned upward and buttoned just below the chin. His Luger P08 fit snugly in a holster embossed with his initials. He carried his padded cap as he left the house, giving the dog, Pope Benedict, a hearty scratch on the head as they passed in the yard, each about his separate business.

Nine of the remaining ten planes had been towed to the edges of the barley field, wheels chocked, some of them with their cowls open, in various states of inspection or repair. One stood waiting at the end of the airstrip, a single mechanic standing at ease beside the propeller.

Gustov pulled on his gloves.

His Fokker Dr.1 was painted in the bold hues of the Voss family heraldry. All three wing decks were orange, as was its nose. The fuselage and tail were azure blue. The Germanic cross—black outlined in white—shared space with the ancestral insignia of a falcon with closed talons. Gustov had resisted the urge to have them paint his name on his bus; a healthy degree of vanity kept a pilot in the sky, but the old gods always batted you down if you took it too far.

His mechanic knew him well enough not to jump hard to attention. Unlike Eldwin, the mechanic understood the odds. He believed that flyers' lives were too short to bullshit them.

"Have you eaten lunch?" Gustov asked as he reached the plane.

"Don't worry about me, Captain. I'll grab a biscuit and coffee later on."

Gustov looked around the sky. "Couldn't ask for better weather."

The mechanic knew he didn't need to comment on the climate. "I touched every single piece of this aircraft after you returned from patrol this morning. It won't fail you."

Gustov fastened his cap to his head. A thick, padded band ran around the crown. Flaps covered his ears. He tied the laces under his chin. "I depend on many people to help me do my job correctly and efficiently every day. But I truly trust only one of them. Thank you."

"The pleasure is mine, Captain. Give the Brit one on the chin for me."

Gustov nodded, mounted the wing, and put himself into his bird of prey.

****

Alec took only three paces into the house before he saw his sister. Her photograph rested in a frame of fine silver filigree atop a fireplace mantel. He'd never seen that picture before; she was laughing, like someone who'd just won a prize at a holiday fair.

Alec was aware that Ellenor was speaking to the middle-aged gentleman who'd answered the door, but they spoke in German, allowing him to fall completely into the image.

He glanced away from his sister's face only briefly. Ellenor and the man with the neatly parted hair were joined by another fellow who had the meek demeanor of a manservant or butler or something along those lines. Whatever role he played here, he was thin and wore a faded frock coat, like a schoolmaster from a Dickens novel. He stood a few feet away and listened as Ellenor spoke in the guttural Hun tongue, presumably explaining who she was and why Alec had come.

Alec returned to the photograph. Nearby were other images: Sarah and her gallant husband, Stefan, dressed like royalty and posing stiff-backed for the camera; the two of them pretending to arm-wrestle; Stefan by himself beside a large factory press. Alec drifted toward the pictures, alarmed by how much he missed this woman. How had he ever let her go? If he had moved here to Germany with her, as she had wanted him to do, would he even now be a happy civilian, gamely going about the Weller family business?

"Alec."

He took the framed portrait from the mantel. He knew a little about photography, as he'd been trained in the use of battlefield cameras that were mounted on planes. But the man who'd captured his sister in this moment of joy was either very talented or very lucky. She looked timeless. Radiant, even. He remembered when they were kids and she'd stolen Mum's scissors and given Alec the worst haircut in the Western hemisphere.

"Alec."

He blinked forcefully. Somewhat embarrassed, he returned the picture to its place, then turned to see Ellenor looking at him all wrong. Her cheeks were drained of color.

The words *What's wrong?* would not move from his mouth. They hung there behind his teeth, refusing to be made real.

Ellenor stared directly at him. Tears filled her eyes but didn't fall.

He swallowed the words and managed something less direct. "Who is this man?"

"He...he is Sarah's father-in-law. Stefan's father. His name is Klaus."

Alec flicked his eyes at him. Klaus, fists in the pockets of his checked vest, looked at the floor.

Alec wanted to grab this Klaus Weller and shout in his face, but he remembered himself, stepped forward, and extended a hand. "Alec Corbin-Dawes, at your service."

The man shook, his hand old and hard. He said a single word in English: "Hello."

Ellenor opened her mouth, closed it, and when the single tear let go and ran down to her chin, Alec knew that everything was lost.

He took both of her hands in his. "Ellenor, please. Tell me that my sister is all right."

Ellenor, very slowly, stepped into him and put her face against his chest.

"Ellenor, whatever you need to say—"

"Sarah is dead."

When Alec was one day away from reporting to the Royal Flying Corps for his first morning as a servant to His Majesty's wartime whims, he finally completed the dollhouse he'd started building for Sarah when they were only ten years old. She would not need it, now that it was finished. She was a woman and had given her dolls away. But a brother kept his promise, however belated it might be.

Ellenor put her arms around his waist and pulled herself into him. "It happened four months ago." Her voice fractured. "Klaus had no way of sending a letter to let you know."

The dollhouse had been a damn excellent bit of woodworking, if Alec said so himself. The little balsa-wood dinette chairs had been his favorite, but the *pièce de résistance* was the tiny chandelier made from bits of colored glass.

"Klaus isn't well," Ellenor whispered. "He hasn't been the same since it happened. He loved her."

"*I* love her, goddammit."

"I know. I'm sorry."

He wanted to cry, but right now he was too angry, because Klaus was lying. Klaus Weller was a dirty German pig who was lying through his black Boche teeth.

Ellenor must have felt his rage, his trembling, his sudden fever. She hugged him closer.

Alec did not return her embrace. "*How*?"

Ellenor sucked up the snot in her throat. "An explosion."

"A *what*? Some kind of factory accident?" Now the lie was becoming farfetched. What kind of shit was Klaus trying to shovel on him? "What the hell are you talking about?"

Ellenor withdrew just enough to look up at him, her eyelashes wet with tears. "Klaus says that Sarah was…"

"Was what?"

"A member of the free-shooters."

"Who the bloody hell are the free-shooters?"

"I don't know. That's what he said. Alec, please, let's just—"

He shoved her away. Two strides brought him toe to toe with Klaus, but the bent-up German wouldn't look at him. "Sir, I would suggest you explain yourself straightaway, before I take this to a place from which you might not recover."

"He doesn't speak English."

"Then translate. *Now*. How did my sister die?" It burned his throat to say it. He could hardly see straight, his heartbeat pounding behind his eyes. "*Speak*."

Ellenor hastily relayed the question, and she spoke over Klaus while he replied. "Sarah was meeting with friends from the Magny district in a bar after hours. Operatives from the High Command…destroyed the building with grenades."

Alec shook his head over and over again. Another lie. "No, no. It couldn't have happened like that. Sarah was a *bookkeeper*."

"I'm sorry."

"Ask him why. What was she doing there?"

Klaus, now struggling against tears of his own, accepted a handkerchief from his butler. He explained as best he could, and Ellenor said on his behalf, "The people at the secret meeting were what the French call *Franc-tireurs*, or free-shooters. They were…guerilla combatants."

"Yes, that's rich. My sister is a highly dangerous insurgent." He laughed, and it sounded like a shriek when it left his throat. "Sarah has never held a gun in her life."

"Klaus believes that his son was one of their leaders. After Stefan died of smallpox, Sarah became more involved in the movement."

"The *movement*?"

"Many of the Messines consider themselves more French than German."

"And they're...what? Playing around at being amateur subversives?"

"I don't know."

"And they were assassinated for plotting treason in a pub?"

"I don't know."

"*Stop saying that.*"

"Then stop treating me like the enemy!" Face red, she pointed at him. "Sarah has passed away, Alec, and I am so, so sorry about that. I ache for you." She pointed at herself. "But it's not my fault." She pointed at Klaus. "And it's not his fault. If you can just take a step back—"

Alec lunged through the front door and slammed it behind him.

The afternoon sun was not his friend. He struck off between two random buildings, keeping to the shadows until he found a dark corner strewn with refuse, where he sank down and put his face in his hands.

The best thing about the dollhouse, though, was not its chandelier. Even though Sarah outgrew the imaginary games she once played in that unfinished house, she always kept it in her room, even when she was as old as eighteen. That was the best thing, that she loved it beyond its usefulness just because her brother

151

had built it.

Alec cried.

He had dozens of things he needed to tell her. Hundreds, really. They were twins; she kidded him about her being one minute older; they were supposed to die on the same day. What had gone wrong? The goddamn war had gone wrong.

Ellenor appeared at the corner, looking around. When her gaze found Alec, she gathered a visible breath before approaching.

Alec wanted her to leave him alone. But at the same time, he didn't. He wanted her beside him. Like her, everything he had was now gone. Did Sarah even have a grave marker? Had Klaus buried her? Was there a funeral? Did anyone know her well enough to say anything over her body that had any meaning at all?

Her body.

He screwed his eyes shut as tightly as he could.

Ellenor sat down and put her arm around him.

Alec leaned into her. How Sarah would have enjoyed meeting Ellenor Jantz. Oh, they would have made quite a pair, each too stubborn to know better. Alec thought of one and let the other cradle him there in the alley, bits of old newsprint fluttering in the air.

After a long time, Ellenor said, "We need to get up."

Alec swallowed. He didn't want to get up. He wanted to strike his own skull against the cracked wall behind him until the pain became moot.

"I know you don't want to eat. Or to sleep. Or to do anything but sit here. I understand that, and I wish there were something I could do. But we need to go indoors. We don't want anyone to ask questions. We can't stay here in this alley."

Alec saw the logic in that but didn't give a shit.

"You don't have to talk to Klaus," she said. "I'm sure he has a room you can use. It's a big house. You can shut the door and stay there for days if you want. I won't blame you. But it's not safe for us here. You don't speak German, and I'm dressed like a man."

He knew as much, but again, he wouldn't have cared if the local police rounded the corner and harassed him for identification papers he didn't possess. Let them throw him in jail. He could abide in a dark room for the rest of his life. What difference did it make now?

"Alec, come on." She took his arm.

Fine. He didn't care either way. He struggled to his feet, eyes wet, throat ablaze. He thought of the four fifty-pound bombs strapped to Hildegard's belly. Perhaps he'd fly over whatever these assholes valued most and blow it straight to hell, along with whoever he could manage to catch in the flames.

Ellenor led him back to the house. A room with a door he could lock behind him sounded like the only thing that might prevent him from screaming. He needed dark solitude.

Klaus gave it to him. He directed his butler to show Alec upstairs and to a spare bedroom in the corner, one with a ceiling that slanted from the angled roofline above.

The butler said something, but Alec closed the door softly in his face and then sat down in the center of the floor.

It didn't matter why Sarah had died, what flag she'd defended, where it happened. Perhaps that would matter tomorrow. Perhaps not. Twins were supposed to die together. She'd let him down.

Alec Corbin-Dawes curled up on his side and wept.

Chapter Eighteen

His fuel tank nearly dry, Gustov grunted his relief when Metz appeared. He'd flown most of the way in a trance, letting the Fokker have its nose the way a rider did with a fine horse. The airstrip was on the near side of the city, five hundred meters from where an observation balloon served as sentry to warn the citizenry of an attack...which was foolish, in Gustov's opinion, as half the population was culturally French and unlikely to be targeted by the home country of their fathers. Still, one could never be too careful.

He flew a low-altitude circle around the city, left wings dipped slightly so that he could peer over the side in search of the stolen aircraft. He saw nothing on the first pass and didn't have fuel to waste on a second. So he cut the engine, glided, and landed without event just as the sun was going down.

They were not expecting him. Nor did they know his name or rank, which suited him fine, as he was in no mood to explain himself to the two mechanics who rushed to meet him as he climbed down from the wing. He asked the way to their commanding officer. He kept his meeting with the CO as brief as possible, answering the man's questions before asking one of his own.

Yes, it was true that a British agent was at large. No, Gustov didn't know his name or his intentions. Yes to this and no to that, and all the while Gustov couldn't help but feel that the Englander was moving farther away with every passing second.

Then Gustov asked his only question: "Can you direct me to Avenue Foch?"

Dusk settled over the city by the time he climbed from the motorbike's sidecar and dismissed the driver. The bike chugged away, coughing fumes. Gustov had only this street name and nothing more. That narrowed his search to several hundred structures and several thousand people.

He smiled to himself.

His vanity had led him here, of course, and with that smile he called out his own arrogance and shook his head. He'd allotted himself precisely twenty-four hours to pursue the Englander, having left Mier in charge of the squadron in his absence. By this time tomorrow, he needed to be landing at Father's manse, whether he had located his quarry or not.

A sooty-faced lamplighter no more than twelve years old parked a wooden stool at the corner gaslight and brought it to life. In its light, Gustov saw a steel sign mounted to the bricks of the nearest building: CAFÉ LINDSEY. If you wanted to begin a search in a strange city—any kind of search, really—you always started at the local tavern.

Once inside, where German and French were spoken interchangeably, along with a smattering of Alsatian, Swiss-German, and Swabian-German, Gustov ordered a beer and sat between two stalwart lads who were not old enough to be drinking but did so copiously. Above them on the wall was a stag head with an antler rack of mythic dimensions, like something Beowulf might have felled. Old men played darts and older men played dominoes. The piano was dreadfully out of tune.

Gustov asked about Englishmen. Were there any around? No, they told him, all the Tommies were out in the scrap, humping their rucksacks through the mud. No one here knew of any man from Britain, but they had plenty to say of the quality of British food. The bartender, who'd lost an eye while fighting for his country's imperial interests in the Boxer Rebellion, said to him, "Everything they eat across the Channel is boiled to death in steam, then covered in a watery white sauce made of wallpaper paste."

Gustov could respond to that only with a laugh and several swallows of beer.

How many taverns lined this street? It was going to be an interesting night.

****

At half past three in the morning, Ellenor woke when someone entered her room.

She'd spent the evening speaking with Klaus. Though he didn't press her for her story, she told him nearly everything, from the crash landing on the hill to the trading away of her honey bee pendant for a quilt to keep her warm. There was little reason to lie to him, as he knew that Alec was Sarah's brother and therefore a Briton here without permission. Klaus would not reveal them to the authorities—or so she hoped.

The only other resident of the house was Klaus's longtime attendant, Uli, who prepared a dinner of braised cabbage and hot potato salad. Ellenor's hunger surprised her. She placed a tray outside Alec's room and knocked on the door but wasn't surprised when he didn't answer. Holding her own sorrow at bay, she

157

listened to the radio news update with Klaus after dinner and then permitted Uli to draw her a bath. As upset as she was, she was not about to deny the glory of hot water and soap, even if it was wartime soap with no scent.

She returned to her small room to find that Uli had placed a selection of sleeping gowns on the narrow bed; she suspected these garments had once belonged to Sarah Weller, which made her simultaneously grateful and sad. She knew she wouldn't sleep, but the weight of the last few days pressed down upon her, and she plunged into her dreams...

Now, hours later, she sat straight up, a gasp trapped in her throat. A figure in her doorway was silhouetted by the candle it held.

"*Get the hell out,*" she hissed in English, too dazed and afraid to remember otherwise.

"I apologize," Uli said in German. "I would not have disturbed you, madam, if it were not a matter of urgency."

She thought of Alec. What had he done? "Is Alec all right?"

"Please, madam, follow me. Your friend is fine. I've already awakened him. He's waiting for us downstairs. We must hurry."

"Hurry?" It didn't make sense. Yet she knew this was not a piece of the dream she'd been enjoying, the one about boats and parasols and languid river rides. "I'll be out in a moment."

Uli left without another word.

Ellenor dressed quickly in clothes he'd provided. In the lamplight, it was hard to see much of the outfit save that it was far more ladylike than what she'd been wearing when she arrived. The fit was somewhat large for her but not so much as to be uncomfortable. She was wearing a dead woman's clothes.

Ignoring that for now, she joined Uli in the hallway. He led her downstairs, then into the parlor, where French doors stood open to the warm night air. Alec waited there, framed against the dark sky.

She hugged him before she could scold herself for her lack of decorum.

He held her tightly, hungrily, and then let her go. He said softly, "Thank you."

"Are you...I mean, are you going to be...?"

"Hard to say, old girl. I hope so."

"What's going on? Why are we here?"

"Haven't the foggiest."

Uli brushed past them. "This way."

Ellenor's pulse hadn't settled since she was torn from sleep. The down-filled mattress had absorbed her, and now—the night air on her cheeks—she realized that whatever intrigue Alec had drawn her into was not quite over yet.

They followed Uli into the garden. The large space was bordered by the house on one side and a tall hedgerow on the other three, completely enclosing the lawn. There were no lights other than Uli's candle, which he shielded with his hand. The dark shape of a gazebo appeared.

Ellenor walked beside Alec, her new pleated skirt rustling against her boots; she wore the knee-high Wellingtons, as Uli hadn't provided any footwear when he'd laid out her clothes.

Uli placed the candle on the gazebo railing. "I'll be in the parlor."

"Wait," Ellenor said. "You're leaving?"

"I won't be far."

"What's happening?"

He kept walking, disappearing into the house.

Ellenor turned back around and was about to say something frantic to Alec when she realized they were not alone. She sensed it. Someone stood just beyond the limit of the candle's glow, concealed in the darkness before the tall shrubs.

She found Alec's hand and interlaced her fingers in his.

A dog barked far away. Night bugs hummed.

"Who are you?" Ellenor said, her voice firm.

Alec gave her hand a squeeze. "We know you're there," he said. "I'm in no mood for drama or idiotic games, so either show your face or let me go back to bed."

Seconds passed.

A woman stepped from the shadows and drew back her hood.

"Hello, little brother," Sarah said.

Chapter Nineteen

Alec threw himself at his sister. He enveloped her with his body, and they both went down to the gazebo floor. He pushed his face into the hollow of her neck and welcomed the tears that leaked through his closed eyes. He gripped her cloak in fingers like claws and inhaled the scent of her fiercely, as if trying to pull her into his lungs.

Sarah, gripping him just as tightly, laughed and cried at the same time.

Alec was born again there on that floor. This was true salvation, not the kind they peddled in the sanctuaries of the Church of England, but a physical sensation of being saved from Hell.

"You're...crushing me," Sarah whispered.

Alec withdrew and tugged her into a sitting position. He wanted to stare at her, just to be sure. The candle was not bright enough. "Is this real?"

"Keep your voice down," she scolded him.

"He said you died."

"I'll tell you everything, but not here."

"Klaus told me that *to my face*."

"Because he believes it. He doesn't know."

"But his man Uli brought me here to you."

"Uli knows. He's one of us."

"One of who?"

"Later, I promise," she said quietly. "So...this must

be Ellenor."

Alec glanced back to see Ellenor watching the two of them, a look of wonder on her face that gave him a good idea of how he likely looked himself. Then he turned back at his sister. "How do you know that?"

"Uli told me. She helped you?"

"I wouldn't be here if not for her. I'd probably be interred in a German prison."

Sarah nudged him away, and Alec reluctantly released her. She got to her feet and extended her hand to Ellenor. "I'm Sarah Weller."

"Ellenor Jantz."

"Well met, Ellenor Jantz. We need to go. All of us. But I want to say thank you for saving the simpleton who is my brother."

"He doesn't seem so simple to me."

Sarah seemed pleased by that. "No, he is not. And apparently he's gone to extraordinary lengths to find me, so perhaps I should be more polite."

Alec stood up. He felt like he might be knocked over again by undiluted joy, so he steadied himself on a gazebo post. "What the devil's going on here, sis?"

"Follow me, and I'll show you." She put on her hood and turned toward a thin gap in the hedges.

Alec caught her by the wrist. "Are you all right? Really?"

She smiled in the candlelight. "I am now. With you here, we might just have a shot."

"A shot at what?"

"Winning." She disappeared through the bushes.

Alec stood there, processing it, his fingertips shaking.

Ellenor slipped by him. "Come on." She followed

Sarah into the unknown.

Alec forced himself to get moving. The proverb he was thinking of was the one about the cocked hat. That's where his plans had been thrown. He'd come here with the intention of outracing a bombing attack and hurtling through the smoke with his rescued twin. And now he found himself getting scratched in the chin by shrubbery in the middle of the night as he raced after her.

Alec became a figure in the dark, moving through streets that lacked all context for him. He moved stride for stride with Ellenor, hurrying from one corner to the next, always swaying toward the shadows. Metz felt empty, abandoned. Even the bakers had yet to rise to stoke their ovens. Trash fluttered along the cobblestones like low-flying bats.

Sarah led them to a stable and tack house, a hulking concrete building where no horses lived. With the advent of the automobile, structures like this had been converted to other purposes. This one had become a crude storage facility, the horse stalls full of crates and rolls of telegraph wire. Sarah moved through the lightless building with confidence until she came to a door mostly hidden behind a stack of cavalry saddles. She rapped four times on the door. A bolt slid back from the other side, and the door opened, revealing even deeper darkness beyond.

She turned back to Alec. "Almost there." She passed through the portal.

Ellenor gave him a slight push. "Keep going," she whispered.

"Keep going *where*?" He scowled and trailed after his sister.

After a descent down a set of slick limestone steps, he emerged in a cellar with a barrel ceiling and walls of plastered concrete. Kerosene lamps revealed tables made of doors, a stack of books, outdated military maps, and an assortment of hunting rifles better suited for the farm than the battlefield. In addition to Sarah, two people stood waiting to receive their guests, a man with a face melted by fire and the other with white hair swept back from his forehead and thick eyeglasses balanced on the tip of his nose.

Surveying the room and its contents, Alec realized, almost to the point of laughter, that he was looking at the headquarters of the local resistance movement.

"You've got to be kidding me," he said.

Sarah ignored him. "Roby, Jules, this is my brother, Alec."

They said hello in their French accents, but Alec didn't return their greetings. This was another of his sister's pranks, like the time she got everyone in class to draw dots on their faces and pretend they'd been stricken with the measles. "Sarah, what is this place and what in God's name are you doing here?"

She opened her mouth to explain, but he interrupted her. "Wait. Let me see if I can piece it together." He took a few steps into the room, stopping near a pile of black leather overcoats. "You've all somehow been wronged by the German government, so you formed a fraternity with a secret handshake and grandiose designs to foment rebellion, and this dungeon is your clubhouse where you come to sharpen your knives."

Sarah gave him precisely the look he'd expected. "Don't do this."

"Don't do what? Point out how ludicrous this all seems?"

"Are you quite finished patronizing me?"

"I rather think I'm just getting started, actually."

"Jesus, Alec, you don't have to be such an arse."

"Then explain it to me, sis." He tossed a hand at her. "Please."

The two men, Roby and Jules, stared at Alec in silence.

Sarah seemed at a loss. Alec had embarrassed her. He didn't care. What had she anticipated would happen when she came back from the dead and dragged him down into her clubhouse?

"Whatever this is," Alec said, "you should all give it up while you can still walk away."

Sarah looked on the verge of lashing out, but then, startling everyone, Ellenor stepped forward and said the only thing that mattered: "This time tomorrow, French planes are going to bomb this city, so we either need to evacuate as quickly as possible or find some way to stop it."

****

Ellenor accepted the mug of coffee from a pot that had been heated over a coal-burning stove. The man named Jules had liquid brown eyes behind his considerable lenses, and he brewed the pot with care. Coffee these days might consist of whatever a ration coupon could buy—and that wasn't always coffee beans. Acorn coffee and chicory coffee were often the best that could be found. But this...

"You like?" Jules asked.

She held the heavy mug in both hands. "Incredible."

"Jules is also an ace mechanic and the closest thing we have to a medic," Sarah said, taking a seat beside her. Sarah Corbin-Dawes-Weller—now *there* was a mouthful—stood two inches taller than Ellenor, which put her at around five-ten and solidly in the territory that intimidated most men. Her blonde hair was cropped short and not in any particular style or shape. She had her brother's jaw and broad shoulders, which fit him attractively but looked blockish on the female version of him.

Alec pulled up one of the wooden chairs between Jules and Roby, completing their circle. For a while they had the sense to say nothing to one another, simply enjoying the warmth of the drink in their throats. Ellenor, not for the first time, marveled at the sudden turn her life had taken.

Eventually Sarah said to her, "I do believe that you're wearing my clothes."

"Uli loaned them to me. I hope that's all right."

"Of course. He told me that you helped Alec escape."

Ellenor nodded. "I'm something of an accidental passenger, but I did my part. And you're trying to do yours. But Alec is afraid you might be going about it the wrong way."

"Going about *what* the wrong way?"

"Whatever it is you're doing down here."

"And how do either of you know what we're doing?"

"You're *Franc-tireurs,* are you not? Free-shooters?" She pressed on, sensing that Alec wasn't the only sibling in need of her help. "I can't pretend to know anything about that. I've fired a gun at a human target only once in my entire life, so I have no advice to offer in such matters. But I do know that Alec is risking a court-martial to find you."

Sarah looked at her brother. "A court-martial? Is that true?"

"Not to get all sentimental on you, sis, but I'd charge a machine gun nest for you, armed with only a blunt bayonet."

"I know. I wanted to speak with you, to send a letter, *something*. And I tried. But there is no communication across the border—none. I didn't know what to do except hope that you were staying safe."

"I fly fighter scouts for the RFC, love, so 'safe' isn't really discussed."

"I'd love to hear about that. I really would."

Ellenor saw Alec return to himself, his foul temper replaced by that glitter he always kept not far from his blue eyes. She said, "Uli explained to you about the plane we took from the Germans?"

"He did. And that might be the most daring thing I've ever heard."

"Well, the observer's seat in that plane was meant for you. Alec intended to fly you out of the city before the bombs fall on your family's factory."

"What? You're saying the factory is the target?"

"You manufacture weapon components for the German army, yes?"

"Of course. That's the problem. Ersten Industrien is mass-producing shell casings for artillery rounds. But E.I. is not *my* company. It never was. My father-in-law, Klaus, is the majority owner. In fact, I begged him to turn down the government contracts. I would do anything to stop E.I. from making those damn things.

Roby and I even sabotaged a few of their trucks. So…if you're telling me that the French air service is going to turn the entire building into rubble, then I'm going to count that as the luckiest thing that's happened to us since my late husband started us all down this path."

Alec laughed sarcastically. "Let me get this straight, sis. I was hell-bent on spiriting you out of town before the bombers arrived, charging over here like some kind of Templar knight on his stolen steed, and now it turns out you *want* the bloody factory destroyed?"

"Just because I married a German doesn't mean I want their soldiers killing our boys."

"Fair enough. It's just a hell of an irony, that's all."

Ellenor was glad to hear the change in Alec's tone; he was simply glad to have his sister back, and all the rest was bluster. She watched him for a moment, how he sat there holding his coffee mug by its rim instead of its handle, and then she forced her attention back to Sarah. "But…what about the workers?" she asked.

"What about them?"

"If the building is destroyed—I'm sorry, what was the name of the company again?"

"Ersten Industrien."

"Yes, Ersten. The workers there are in danger. You might be safe, but innocent people will be killed in the attack. We can't let that happen."

"Agreed," Alec said. "But we don't have much time to figure it out. The French planes are due to arrive here at Metz tomorrow before dawn, at approximately four in the morning. We need to make sure that civilians are nowhere near that building."

"Of course," Sarah concurred. "But neither the E.I.

employees nor any random citizen is in danger from an air raid. The bombers will never make it to the factory."

"And why is that?"

"Because ever since the city began turning all of its efforts toward military contracts, it has greatly increased its defenses against the very threat you're describing."

"What do you mean?"

"I assume that your intelligence operatives are unaware of the six anti-aircraft guns that arrived a week ago."

Alec said nothing.

"I thought as much." Sarah turned to the two men sitting quietly beside her. "Roby, can you enlighten us with the details?"

Roby cleared his throat. Half of his face was like a hardened lava flow, the result of some horrific burn. "The Huns call these newly installed anti-aircraft weapons *Fliegerabwehrkanone*, or Flak, for short." Roby's voice was glassy, smooth and hard. "A Flak unit is most effective when several guns fire in sequence. Each shell is timed so that it detonates in the air, sending out a spray of fire and fragments intended to bring down incoming aircraft."

Ellenor looked at Alec. Had he flown through such barrages before?

Roby continued. "The big ninety-millimeter Flaks are supported by nasty little thirty-sevens that work like the American Gatling gun, with rotating barrels that fire flares up to five thousand feet high."

Alec said, "We flyers call those 'flaming onions.'"

"A fitting name," Roby agreed. "The Germans use the term *lichtspucker*, or light-spitter, because the damn thing vomits up fire at such a high rate. And they have ten of them ringing the city in support of half a dozen ninety-millimeter wheeled Flak guns. Throw in an observation balloon, a searchlight unit, and an armored communications bunker, and our fair town is as well-guarded as the Kaiser's latrine."

No one said anything. Ellenor watched Alec, waiting for him to make it all better with a word of wit and a crafty grin, but he looked uncharacteristically grim. She shared his appreciation for the irony of coming here to rescue Sarah only to learn that not only was his sister in no need of saving, she was also desperate to stop the work being done at her own factory.

Ellenor wondered if this was what Josef meant by *bashert*. Probably not.

Sarah broke the silence. "It's like this. The sky over Metz is protected by sixteen different guns, at our last count, plus a reinforced command center. So unless you can get a message back to your friends in France sometime today, every single plane they send will be blown out of the sky."

Chapter Twenty

Gustov woke with a woman on his chest.

In all the ways a man could wake up in the morning, there were perhaps only three that mattered. One: in jail. Two: in a hospital bed. Three: in a lover's arms. The other variations, though many were important, did not indicate such an interesting history.

He slid from beneath her. She purred and slipped back into sleep.

Last night and into the early hours of the black Metz morning, he'd visited five—no, *six*—taverns along Avenue Foch. No one had seen the Englander, nor any foreigners at all, for that matter. These were Messines, a people in love with life and, in an existential way, in love with war. That conflict on the Hindenburg Line not so far away reminded them that they were brothers. Every hour they were free was a gift they longed to share with the men at the Front, soldiers who got so sick with gangrene that their body parts were amputated by field surgeons with wagons for operating rooms. The bar patrons had adored Gustov because he embodied the patriotism they felt only when their country was fighting someone else. They had loved him for his handsome face and for his acumen at cards. They had plied him with drink. When they learned he was an airman, they'd practically fallen to pieces in excitement. None had ever flown in an airplane before. He had borne their endless questions with the patience only a hunter knows.

He swung his feet from the boardinghouse bed.

Shortly before sunrise, he'd found his way here, mostly drunk. But there was not a pilot in this war who was a stranger to drinking until sunrise and then finding sobriety in the clouds on a dawn patrol. Now, only a few hours later, Gustov would have to strap on his holster and continue his investigation. He'd promised Mier and the men that he'd return to Father's farm by late afternoon.

He stood, feeling the warmth spread through his abdominals and lower back, and walked naked to where a stack of folded towels waited near the door. He wrapped his lower body, picked up his travel kit, and left the room in search of coffee, a sink in which to shave, and a toilet, in whichever order they happened to present themselves.

When he returned to his room, dressed and normalized by breakfast, the woman was gone. He tidied the area, paid his bill, and fired himself like an arrow into the neighborhood outside, once again consumed with his mission. Surely someone on this street had seen the Englander. Someone had a story to tell.

Gustov started with a bootblack on the corner, asking his one question while his boots were being buffed. He was prepared to ask it as many times as necessary. He was a man of uncluttered intent. He had not told the woman his name nor asked for hers in return.

****

Alec and Ellenor crept back into Klaus Weller's

house while the world was still dark enough to conceal their passage. They stole up the stairs, whispered a goodnight even though the sun would rise in less than an hour, and disappeared into their respective rooms.

Alec had no intention of sleeping.

He threw himself into the creaking little bed, put his arms behind his head, and gazed up at the slanted ceiling.

He lay there for less than a minute before realizing he needed to speak with Ellenor. The two of them had arranged to meet again with Sarah and her friends at eleven in the morning, only a few hours from now. Roby and Jules represented the entire membership of Sarah's army of revolutionaries. The German *Polizei* had arrested or killed enough malcontents that everyone but those three quixotic fools had gone to ground. And unless he and Ellenor intervened, the *Franc-tireurs* of Metz were going to meet their ruin tomorrow in the dark hours before dawn, and the Spads and Breguet 14s and all the men inside them would leave the aerodrome and never return.

Alec got up, departed his room, went to Ellenor's door, and promptly lost his nerve.

Shit. He'd killed men ten thousand feet above the face of the earth. He'd been the target of hundreds of bullets. And yet his knuckles were frozen in space, two inches from her door.

"Sally forth, old boy." With that, he knocked.

She opened the door almost immediately She'd brushed her long hair.

He whispered, "May I come in?"

She stepped aside without a word. Alec entered.

She'd not yet turned out the oil lamp beside the

bed. Like him, she was not inclined to sleep, not when the bombing raid was scheduled for approximately twenty-four hours from now.

"I'd ask you to sit down, but…" She indicated the lack of chairs between the bed and the cedar chest.

"No worries." Alec dropped to the floor and leaned against the bed as if it were the back of a chair. He patted the space beside him.

After only a moment's hesitation, Ellenor lowered herself down to her designated spot.

"Hell of a night, eh?" he said.

"It's one surprise after the next. How's your hand?"

He held it up and unwrapped the bandage. The wound was red and puckered but no longer throbbed. "At least you didn't shoot any fingers off."

"I panicked. I thought you were going to hurt me."

"I'm sure it will leave a fascinating scar." He put his hand down. "Do you like her?"

"Sarah? I hardly know her."

"Apparently I don't really know her, either. All this free-shooter business…" He wasn't even sure what to say about it.

"Well, I suppose the question of how to fly your sister to France has been answered. She doesn't intend to go at all. She wants to stay and fight."

"Fight and get killed, yes, and as much as I'd love to boast of a martyr in the family, I'm not going to let that happen."

"Unless we plan on kidnapping her, our only other option is to stay and help."

"Then we'll stay and help."

"But you heard what Roby said. All those big guns

are placed around the city. How bad is that, exactly? You know far better than I do…can the French planes make it through all that?"

"They'll be slaughtered. I've experienced anti-aircraft fire in the worst possible way. We call it 'ack-ack' or 'Archie.' The shells are set to some kind of mechanical timer so they explode at a predetermined moment after launching. And when they do, they spew out a mess of fire and little steel fragments. Flying through ack-ack is like…um…"

"Like moving through a cloud of angry bees?"

He smiled. "Quite."

"So…is there any way to get word of this to the French? Can we warn them?"

"We haven't the time."

"Even in our plane?"

"Hildegard is a dear, and I've already fallen madly for her, but as soon as we approach the Front, her German markings will get us shot down by our own allies, and I don't think painting a Union Jack on her wings is the answer."

"Then what do we do?" She narrowed her eyes, suddenly suspicious. "You've already thought of a plan, haven't you?"

"What makes you say that?"

"That look on your face."

"I don't have a look." He couldn't help but grin again. Sarah was alive, and now Alec sat on the floor beside a woman who compelled him in a way he was only now admitting to himself. He was in rare spirits. "I'm famous for my bold plans, you know."

"Certainly. The last one almost got me killed."

"You're still alive, aren't you?"

"I'm wearing another woman's skirt because I've only one change of clothes to my name. I may be alive, but I'm also destitute."

"That makes us two of a kind. But we'll need to worry about our wardrobe later."

She shifted just enough that she was facing him. "I'm listening."

Alec paused for a few seconds. His idea might not sound so credible if he spoke it aloud.

"Say it," she said.

"As you wish." He nodded, mostly to himself. "Dear Hildegard is carrying a quartet of fifty-pound bombs in her egg basket. Those ack-ack emplacements are located outside the city, away from civilians. I plan to get her in the sky and bomb the shit out of those guns."

Ellenor's eyes widened at the thought. "You can do that?"

"Hildegard was born for it. And I was born to fly her."

"That's sounds awfully dramatic. Will it work?"

"It *should*. I mean, yes, of course it will work. But, um…"

"What?"

"Well, I have one small problem."

"Yes?"

"The lever that releases the bombs isn't located in the pilot's cockpit."

She slowly realized what he was implying. "The observer drops the bombs."

He winked at her. "Indeed."

Chapter Twenty-One

"I can't do that," Ellenor said.

"Why not?"

"I don't know anything about bombs."

"I'll teach you."

"Teach Roby. He looks rugged enough. He was probably a soldier before he was injured. I'm sure he's far better suited to the task than I am."

Alec shook his head. "For one thing, Roby has likely never been off the ground in his life, and he'll puke out his guts as soon as we're at elevation. We can't afford a practice run to test his constitution, and I can't take the chance he's fit for the job. Secondly, and far more importantly, I don't want him up there with me. I want you."

Ellenor had no rebuttal for that. No flippant word. No bit of banter to deflect his gaze. His words moved her. She and Alec were in this together, however it turned out. Ellenor's trust in him was disproportionate to the amount of time she'd known him. The day she'd met him, he'd said one simple thing as he lay bleeding: *I have to find her*. Yet now that he'd reached Sarah, his motivations had changed, and Ellenor's had changed along with them.

"You shouldn't say things like that," she told him.

"In wartime, one speaks only the truth."

"And what if we weren't at war?"

177

"Oh, I suppose I'd skirt the subject indefinitely, knowing me."

Ellenor imagined herself up there with him, taking to the skies under the cover of a new moon, banking hard to the left and tipping the release lever, listening to a bomb whistle as it fell...

"What are you thinking?" he asked.

"What will we do after this?"

"What do you mean?"

"Let's say we convince Sarah to go forward with this plan of yours tonight and by some miracle we succeed in not dying. What happens next?"

"Find a bottle of champagne and celebrate?"

"While we're flying away? We won't be able to land here again. The military at all the nearby posts will rush in to see who was responsible. Once we're in the air, win or lose, we'll have to keep going."

"Hmmm. I suppose you're right. We'll make sure to take on plenty of petrol."

"But where will we go?" she pressed, knowing he hadn't considered it. He might have had a life back home in Derby, but did he expect her to get on a steamship and sail back to America? Nothing was waiting for her there. Everything she had was in front of her.

After a while he said, "I wish I had an answer for you. I had imagined that Sarah and I would land safely back in France, then make our way to a port somewhere, perhaps Calais, and use some of Sarah's money to pay for passage to England. I'd report to an RFC base and confess my story so as not to be branded a deserter for the rest of my life, and then I'd face whatever punishment they gave me. They'd never let me near an airplane again, but it would've been worth it. Now none of that is happening. I'll talk to Sarah, see what she wants to do. All I know for certain is that I'm not going anywhere without you, if you don't mind."

She kept her hands folded safely in her lap. "I don't mind at all."

When they heard Klaus stirring downstairs, they washed and joined him for breakfast. He was a man whose son had died of smallpox and daughter-in-law was presumed dead, and he wore those burdens. Ellenor saw it in the way he moved, like a man carrying a yoke across his shoulders. Sarah was cruel to let him live like this. Ellenor intended to confront her about it when next they met.

Uli prepared a simple breakfast of *Müesli* and milk. Alec—freshly scrubbed—assisted with the tea, while Klaus read a newspaper that was six days old; the plain cereal was due to a lack of fresh fruit, and the outdated paper to a shortage of newsprint. Delivery trucks came less frequently by the week. Ellenor found herself making an effort to talk to Klaus about anything that seemed to interest him. He enjoyed visiting the local *Kientopp,* a storefront cinema, though he complained that most films were preceded by at least one reel of war propaganda. Ellenor ached for him, as half of his sorrow could be alleviated if Uli would just tell him the truth. She developed a grudge against Sarah that she vowed to resolve before noon.

Klaus Weller put on his hat and left for the factory, telling Ellenor they could stay as long as they liked. He enjoyed their company, even if his taciturn demeanor indicated otherwise.

Watching through the drapes as he made his way

down the walk, Ellenor suspected she would never see him again. Her life had become a series of interludes.

When they were ready, Uli led them out again, taking a different route to the hulking stable building and avoiding contact with those they passed along the way. The morning was clear and vibrant; when the afternoon arrived, it would be hot. A church steeple with brass trim reflected the sun like a lighthouse.

A lookout was now posted outside the stable. He was a cripple, nonchalant, reading a disintegrating copy of *The Metamorphosis* with a jar half full of *pfennig* coins beside him. Uli dropped in a handful of change, and the man did not even glance up. Ellenor noticed the string mostly covered in straw a few inches from where he sat. She knew the other end of that line was connected to a bell downstairs.

A few minutes later, they were underground again, where Roby field-stripped an Enfield rifle and Jules waited with his arms crossed near Sarah, like a court bodyguard within reach of his queen.

"Good morning," Sarah said. "I hope you were able to get a couple of hours of sleep. Let's have a seat. We need to work this out. If you're right about the timing of the raid, we have a little over sixteen hours to find a solution."

They gathered in wooden chairs.

Ellenor didn't want to miss her chance. She spoke first, looking at Sarah. "Why do you let Klaus go on thinking you're dead? Do you not trust him to keep your secret?"

Sarah seemed as if she'd been expecting the question. "I hear what you're saying. It's on my mind almost every day. But it's not Klaus so much as the people he knows. He's a successful businessman. He has friends who are bankers, barristers, politicians, generals. I can't risk telling him the truth, because he might choose to confide in the wrong person."

"So you let him live in misery?"

"If they know I'm alive, I'm a danger to him. This is the only way I can keep him safe."

"I don't think anyone is safe anymore," Ellenor said. "We just have to hope for luck, or for a hand to hold. It's all too precarious to let him go on living like that. You need to tell him."

"Or what? You'll tell him yourself?"

The thought had occurred to her. Sarah must have seen that in her face.

Sarah acquiesced with a nod. "Let's concentrate on the problem at hand. If we make it through the night, I'll find a way to speak with Klaus. I promise."

Alec said, "Better take her up on that promise, old girl. My dear sister may have her faults, but I've never known her to break a vow."

"I believe you." Ellenor didn't know what prompted her, but she stood up and held out her hand. Maybe shaking would make it permanent and real.

Sarah rose and clasped her hand in return and then did something that surprised everyone in the room: she pulled Ellenor into a close embrace.

As Ellenor returned the hug, Sarah whispered in her ear: "*My brother is smitten.*"

Before Ellenor could process this, Sarah withdrew to her seat and said with authority, "So let's find some way of sticking it to these Boche bastards, shall we?"

****

With fifteen hours remaining, Alec studied the map

they'd drawn on a long length of butcher's paper. The nests of the big ninety-millimeter weapons were marked with circles drawn by Jules with an architect's precision. The guns were positioned far enough from the city that streetlamps would not illuminate them at night, so they could remain mostly invisible in the dark. This also meant, however, no risk of civilian casualties when Alec and Ellenor dropped their bombs. The command center—a half-buried block of reinforced cement—hunched in the shadow of the Cathedral of Saint Stephen as if embarrassed to be there.

"I hear the Frenchies are on the verge of mutiny," Roby said.

"The infantry's in bad shape," Alec confirmed, studying the schematic. "They're sick of being ordered to go over the top and be shredded by happy Huns with machine guns. Can't say I blame them."

"And the air service?"

"A different story. Morale's a bit stronger at the aerodromes."

"Why is that?" Sarah asked.

"I suppose we have a dissimilar view of the conflict."

"You're fighting against the same enemy as the infantry, aren't you?"

Alec's smile contained no mirth. It felt like a cold, almost bitter thing on his face. "We flyers don't know the real war, because we don't know the smell."

"What does that mean?" Sarah asked. "What smell?"

Alec wondered how much he should say. "It's like this. Boys and horses have been dying in the same trenches for three years. There are layers of them stuffed into the muck by now, their skulls and skin the same color as the mud. They died to take fifty yards of territory that some other platoon had lost the week before. They can't be buried properly. It's all slime and shit out there. So they sink into the mire. A month later, when an entrenching team is sent to dig a new communications tunnel in knee-high water, they find the bodies, chaps that look just like them, their chests full of happy little medals and their entrails swimming with worms. The constant smell can drive a man mad." He ran a hand through his blond hair. "Flyers know about dying. But we don't know about war."

Ellenor shuddered visibly at this description. Roby nodded and said simply, "Aye."

"Back to the matter at hand," Sarah said, attempting to keep them on task. She touched the map. "The French squadron arrives over the city early tomorrow morning, before sunup. To clear the way for them, we're facing two different threats that require two different solutions."

"The ack-ack *and* the bunker," Alec said.

"Correct. For the sake of argument, let's say the two of you are a smashing success and manage to take out most of the guns. The command center is sunk halfway in the ground. It's made of concrete and steel. You can't count on destroying it from the air, and there's no way that Roby and Jules and I can force our way inside. And that means the wireless radio will alert every German soldier within a hundred-kilometer radius as soon as your first bomb hits the ground. They'll get planes in the air from all directions. If the radio operators remain in that bunker, it will take a miracle to keep you in one piece."

"You don't think a bomb can penetrate that place?"

"For one thing, you don't have a bomb to spare. It will take all four if you hope to eliminate enough of the anti-aircraft weapons to make a difference, simply because they're positioned too far apart from one another. But aside from that, no, I don't think you can blast your way through even if you had spare munitions."

"Then what's the point of all this, sis?"

"The point is to save the French planes so they can destroy the factory, which you can still accomplish."

"Sure, at the expense of our own lives. There are probably half a dozen *Jastas* within a short flight of this city, and if the radio men are allowed to transmit, half the *Luftstreitkräfte* will be on top of Ellenor and me before we get five miles away. Don't you have some local rabble you can rouse to assault the bunker?"

"Look around. This is what we have."

"Well, I'm not quite sure how I feel about a suicide mission."

"We'll call it off, find another way."

"There *is* no other way."

Sarah threw up her hands. "What would you have us do, Alec? Do you want those French pilots to fly into a deathtrap? And if E.I. keeps mass-producing shells, how many other deaths will be on our hands?" She sighed, the frustration causing her shoulders to sag. "At the same time, I don't want you hurt, either of you, so as long as that bunker is occupied, I won't support this mission."

No one seemed to know what to say after that. Roby had carved a scale model of one of the German guns, and he turned it over in his hands. Jules swished coffee in his mug. Alec stared at his sister, wishing she'd never met Stefan Weller and moved to this wretched place.

"Can I tell you about the bees?" Ellenor said into the silence.

They all looked at her.

"I don't belong here," she began. "In fact, the very idea that I'm sitting here in this basement, discussing ways to blow things up and save lives, is so far removed from who I am that it's like I'm back in the children's room again at Father's farm, reading them a story of a woman from another world. So all I can do is talk about what I know best." She gathered her thoughts and continued. "When you're a beekeeper, you regularly find yourself facing fifty thousand armed warriors who are willing to die for their queen. The only way to stay safe when you're working the hive is to confuse them all with smoke. So the men in that bunker…we smoke them out."

Chapter Twenty-Two

Gustov lost his temper at quarter after twelve that afternoon.

The morning had been a waste. He'd stopped by one shop after the next, asked his question, and then moved on. He'd parleyed with pedestrians and chatted war gossip with small-scale merchants selling everything from castor oil to postage stamps. He'd purchased trinkets in hopes of bribing shopkeepers, only to give those ornaments away to passing children. He ate a nondescript midday meal at a café in which he was the only customer. He asked the woman in the apron if she had served anyone with a British accent or any woman fitting Ellenor's description.

Back outside in the street, he heard someone say, "Piss off, flyboy."

This comment was so out of context that Gustov almost walked away without noticing. He was experiencing a pleasant if unproductive day among pleasant if uninspired people, and to be called a name was startling.

He stopped, turned. "I beg your pardon?"

"I told you to leave us alone." The man wore a faded, shapeless work shirt and hobnail boots without laces. He spoke his German with a French lilt, revealing his loyalties. Not everyone in Metz appreciated the multicultural richness their city enjoyed. Most men and women were content, but cretins abounded.

Gustov relaxed. There was no threat here, only poverty and blame. "Good afternoon."

"You can take your 'good afternoon' and shove it sideways up your ass crack."

A military man, Gustov had heard far more original curses. "We haven't met, yet clearly I've offended you."

"Every kraut in an airplane offends me."

"A French partisan, I see."

"France has got nothing to do with it." He came closer, his eyes red and haunted, his cheeks chapped. Only now did Gustov realize that the man wore the remains of an enlisted soldier's uniform shirt. "You pompous shit-eaters in your fancy planes strafed my platoon at Verdun because you didn't have the balls to take up a rifle and face us like men. That's no decent way to fight, plugging away at helpless sods on the ground who can't even lift a finger to stop you."

"I wasn't at Verdun. You have my condolences for your loss."

"This war is going to be won or lost on the ground, by real warriors, and not by a group of fairies in planes painted like whores paint their faces."

Gustov neared his breaking point. He felt the change inside himself and welcomed it.

"I'd rather share a cigarette with an infantry man from either side than a flyboy," the Frenchman said, spittle on his lips. "What makes you any better than us? What gives you the right to miss out on frostbite and Weil's disease and all the goddamn fleas?"

A few hours ago, Gustov would have patted this disgruntled fellow on the shoulder and continued about his business. But his sense that his quarry was escaping had affected him in a primitive way. "Are you quite finished, sir?"

"I'm just getting started. Look at you. There you stand, dressed like a demigod—but me?" He shrugged "I'm not even worthy of brushing the lint from your uniform." He reached up and flicked the tips of his fingers across an imaginary crumb on Gustov's chest.

Gustov punched him in the throat.

The man gagged instantly, letting out a series of dog-like sounds as he crumpled to his knees. He clutched at his neck, choking.

Gustov grabbed him by the hair. He tightened his fist, getting a good grip of the unwashed strands and shaking the man's skull. While the poor wretch coughed, Gustov glanced around, seeing the faces staring at him. People stopped what they were doing to witness the commotion on the corner. Violence was rare in the city, as the residents were the very young and the very old, with all the hot-blooded types shipped off to the Front. This, then, was something wicked and new.

No longer giving a shit about appearances, Gustov drew his Luger with his free hand and jabbed the barrel into the man's eye. The man yelped, terror flashing through the pain.

"I respect everyone I meet," Gustov explained to him. "It is unfortunate, sir, that you do not hold to similar standards."

The man continued to choke, crying now.

Gustov pressed the gun harder into his eye socket. "If I were to let you go, who is to say that you would learn anything from our colorful encounter?"

The man tried to nod. He begged in between his coughs, whispering, "*S'il vous plaît*," over and over again.

Gustov tightened his fist, causing the man's head to shudder. Hundreds of eyes could not look away from him as the people of Metz stood flatfooted in the street and doorways. Fingers parted curtains in dark windows. Gustov felt their frightened gazes on his face. They did not judge. They feared him. He wanted to give them back their tranquility. He didn't want their impression of him to be how he dealt with insolence from one of their sons.

"Please, sir…"

To hell with it. Gustov shot him.

The bullet blew a soup of bone and red meat from the back of the man's head, splattering the storefront with blood and gray chunks of brain. The sudden report made the onlookers jump; they recoiled in horror, a few of them rushing away, most of them welded in place.

Gustov looked down at the Frenchman, a red puddle spreading across the ground. The man had died instantly, unlike many of the pilots Gustov defeated in the air. Those were honorable men who had not deserved a protracted death as they burned or fell. This rodent had gotten lucky.

Gun in hand, Gustov raised his voice so that his words carried along the street: "I am looking for a man from Britain and a German-speaking American woman with dark hair. Someone here has seen them. I have money for anyone who aids me. You tell me what you know, and I will pay you, no questions asked. But if you have seen that man and woman and *do not* tell me, when I find out, I will come to your home and execute you in front of your family." That last part wasn't true, but he saw its effect on their faces. "I shall be at Café Lindsey awaiting your assistance."

With that, he walked away, quivering with energy. He knew there would be consequences, a visit from the police, a debriefing by High Command, but he'd been assaulted in the line of duty and defended himself. They would not discipline him. In point of fact, most of them feared him, regardless of their rank. The Voss family name traced its influence to the time of the Reformation, and even in this bitter world, where one sowed salt in his enemy's fields and plotted upheavals, names still mattered.

Gustov holstered his sidearm, then retraced his steps as the sun burned across the afternoon sky, every eye on Avenue Foch watching him go.

****

At shortly after two o'clock, fourteen hours before the French planes faced the Flak batteries above Metz, Ellenor sat in a stone room below an abandoned stable and thought again of Sarah's furtive message: *My brother is smitten.*

Leaning forward in her chair with her elbows on her knees and her fingers laced, Ellenor revealed nothing in her demeanor. On the outside, she was an attentive member of the meeting being conducted on a table that had been a door in a past life, its surface cluttered with cups and sketches and smoldering cigarettes. On the inside, she walked a wire like an acrobat anticipating a breeze. Did Alec really feel that way about her? Or was Sarah—who hadn't seen her brother since before the war—misinterpreting his intentions?

"...but our timing will need to be crackerjack," Alec was saying. "Ellenor and I need to be in the sky at the same time you three gas the bastards from their box."

"And we're woefully short on supplies," Roby said. "We aren't prepared for an operation like this. We usually take weeks in the planning stage."

Sarah took up a pen and opened her notebook. "We'll list everything we need to make it happen. You talk, I'll write."

Roby started them off: "If we follow Ellenor's plan, we'll need materials to create the smoke—rags, oil, coal."

"Steel fireboxes and shovels," Jules added.

"An automobile to carry it all," Roby continued, "plus dark clothing."

"And weapons."

"Yes, and that."

Without looking up from her work, Sarah said, "Alec? How about you?"

"Our petrol tank is almost empty. Hildegard is down to a few drops."

Roby pointed to a spot on the map he'd rendered. "We can purchase fuel from the depot here. How much do you need?"

"If I remember correctly from our endless briefings on enemy aircraft, our bird holds around one hundred and seventy liters in her main tank and about fifty in the auxiliary. Can we get that much?"

"This may be wartime, my friend, but money still moves mountains."

"You free-shooters have a financial backer?"

Sarah explained: "My late husband and I put some

191

money away for emergencies. We have enough for what we need tonight."

"Excellent. Assuming you also have access to transportation, Roby and I can take some barrels and make the deal while the rest of you acquire the ingredients for the smoke. That sound all right with you, El?"

Ellenor didn't immediately reply. First of all, he'd called her *El*, which was a new but not unwanted development, and secondly, she realized that after this evening and the early hours of tomorrow morning, however it played out, she would be gone from here forever.

Where would she go?

"I'll help in any way I can," she said, and thought it sounded like a lame reply.

They divided their duties. Alec and Roby would purchase fuel and transport it to where the Rumpler was hidden in the trees; the containers were heavy, and both men would be needed to hoist them. At the same time, Ellenor and Jules would acquire the necessary items to fashion the black smoke that would hopefully drive the radio operators from their post. When both tasks were complete, they'd meet back here at dusk to face the conversation that Ellenor knew Alec was dreading. What would happen after it was all over? Would Sarah stay and fight? Or could Alec convince her to restart her life on safer shores? And if so, how would he get her there?

She had little time to wonder about it. Jules donned a narrow-brimmed hat and escorted her from the cellar, with Sarah remaining behind so as not to be recognized as a woman who was supposed to be dead. Ellenor didn't even have a chance to wish Alec good luck. He and Roby were already gone.

Outside, the afternoon revealed nothing of war. Yes, much of the window glass had been replaced with wooden sheets, and certainly many of the shops closed their doors at odd hours. Yet the sun seemed unaware of all that, determined to warm the skin and push back the gloom.

"We'll cut through here," Jules said, guiding her into an alley under strings of laundry hung between upper-level windows. Jules was sixty years old, with a mane of white hair he wore flattened back from his forehead. His eyes were distorted behind his lenses. He seemed French to his very marrow, his mannerisms and attire distinctly Parisian, but he spoke rarely, performing his role of clandestine scrounger without question. Ellenor wondered what story had brought him into Sarah's circle but didn't have the time to ask. After tonight, he would become one more memory.

For now, though, he was very real. He led her through the city's cobbled streets with little nods of his head, occasionally asking if she wanted to stop for food or rest or a toilet. He eventually led them to a junk dealer whose lean-to marketplace was positioned across the street from a clockmaker's studio that had been turned into a dispensary for ration coupons. Jules introduced the proprietor as Selig.

Ellenor said hello but didn't give her name.

"How have we not met, you and I?" Selig asked her.

"I'm new here."

"And pretty," Selig said, playing his eyes over her.

Jules scowled. "Selig, please, none of that. We've

come for rags. As many as we can stuff into these sacks."

"An odd request."

"It's an odd war."

"I'll agree with you on that one." Over the next twenty minutes they filled the bags with scrap shirts, old cotton strips, worn pillowcases, and wads of burlap. As Selig tied a leather cord around the neck of one of the sacks, he said, "There's been a shooting."

"Anyone I know?" Jules asked.

Selig shook his head. "A vagrant got crossways with a military officer, from what I hear. I wasn't there, but people are on edge, so be careful."

"I'm always careful," Jules said.

Until tonight, Ellenor thought. She'd not been careful for the last five days. Nor would she be careful tomorrow. And the day after tomorrow—if they made it that far—was a horizon too distant to see.

The next items on their list were oil and coal, along with matches and backup matches in case those got wet and failed. Jules let his paranoia unfurl around him, muttering about all the things that could go wrong. The match would fail to light; the *Polizei* would see them; the smoke would have no effect on those inside. He tried to provide options for every contingency, and Ellenor carried the bundles on her back. She thought about Alec. She thought about learning how to drop a bomb from an airplane. She thought about the frames of honey still needing to be harvested from her hives.

"Ready to head back to base and make this happen?" Jules asked when they were done.

"I'm not sure that I am."

He didn't seem to know how to respond to that. "Is

there something I can do to help?"

"Can you stop the world?"

"It's all a little much, isn't it, mademoiselle?"

"May I ask you a question that has nothing to do with any of this?"

"But of course."

"Is it possible to start one's life completely over?"

"In France, all things are possible."

"This isn't France."

He shrugged one shoulder. "Not yet, perhaps. But with your help, who is to say what we can become?"

"The liberation of Metz puts a tremendous burden on my shoulders."

"Something tells me that you're stronger than you would have us believe. Now, enough talk. *Allons-y*." He set off along the street, burdened with fire-making supplies.

Ellenor, gathering herself with an inhale of afternoon air, quickened her step to catch up.

Chapter Twenty-Three

As they drove across the city for petrol to refill Hildegard's tank, Alec said to Roby, "Let me tell you a joke."

"Please do."

The lorry in which they rode was a Marienfelde model with a cramped cab barely big enough for the two of them; their elbows almost touched whenever Roby shifted gears. The vehicle's bed was long and narrow and holding three empty steel drums and the cables that secured them. Alec was six feet tall, and his head nearly bumped the cab's ceiling whenever the wheels struck one of Metz's many holes.

"Here's the story, and I swear it's true," Alec said, bracing himself on the door frame. "The infamous Hun general, Hindenburg, finally catches an Allied slug and dies."

"I like this story already," Roby said.

"I thought you might. Hindenburg unfortunately doesn't go to Hell where he belongs but instead arrives at Heaven and knocks on the gate. However, St. Peter tells him, 'A great military man such as yourself ought to come with a horse.' So Hindenburg goes back to Berlin and reports details of this experience to the Kaiser, who grows angry at how his best man has been treated in the afterlife. 'Saint or no saint,' Kaiser Wilhelm says, 'that Peter should know better than to impose such conditions on a man as mighty as you. Come, I shall speak to him myself.' The two of them fly up to Heaven, but when Peter sees them, he waves his hands madly and shouts, 'Hindenburg, you fool, I told you to come with a horse, not with an ass!'"

Roby wasn't the laughing type, but he managed a coarse chuckle and a satisfied nod.

"That's the best I have today," Alec said. "Too nervous for anything better."

"Nervous about flying tonight?"

"God, no. Flying is the only thing that makes sense. I get up there above everything and watch the toy soldiers plinking at one another…I'd rather be aloft than anywhere else."

"You're not sure about instructing Ellenor in the range-finder?"

"She'll be fine. She's a quick study."

"So what is it, then?"

Alec found it difficult to say aloud. Fate had given him the chance to play the hero, the valiant protagonist in the cockpit of a warbird that would save the lives of French flyers and bring about the ruin of a Hun factory. For what more could a man ever ask?

"You don't have to say anything," Roby told him, guiding the lumbering vehicle around a corner. "A man's business is his own, more so now than ever."

"No, privacy has nothing to do with it. The fact of the matter is that, for the first time in my life, I'm unable to predict what will happen tomorrow."

"No one can see the future but old Romanian crones with cards."

"That's not what I mean. One always has a general idea of what the next day holds. Of course we're surprised by life all the time, but we basically know the workplace we'll visit or the school we'll attend or the home waiting for us when we're done." He stared from the window at the limestone homes tucked up tightly against one another, obvious cracks threatening their foundations. "But when Ellenor and I drop that last bomb and fly away before the German response arrives, I haven't a notion if we'll end up in Switzerland or Italy or Spain."

"You could stay."

"If I land Hildegard and sneak back into the city, the Germans will eventually find her. That can't happen."

"It's not your plane."

"She is now." Alec knew that even if he avoided jail, the RFC would never let him fly again. His life had boiled down to a small handful of goals, one of which was to keep flying.

"You don't have much time to choose a destination."

"Which way is the wind blowing?"

"From the northwest."

"So it will blow us to the Alps, then. Sadly, we won't have the petrol to make it that far."

No sooner had he mentioned fuel than they arrived at a field of rusty tanks, surrounded by a fence topped with razor wire. Though the depot was a civilian facility, it remained under heavy guard. Men bearing mismatched weapons stalked the perimeter. Yellow metal signs posted at every corner read FORBIDDEN in three languages.

Roby conducted business. The transaction was quick and discreet. A moment later, the lorry was rolling through the gate toward the storage tanks, Alec jostling in his seat. That was another fine thing about being in the air: no bloody potholes.

They filled their barrels with few words between them. Alec felt an increasing sense of urgency. He deflected serious topics as part of his nature, but now he couldn't find room for levity. From this point forward, with smelly petrol gurgling into the steel drums as he waited impatiently, he would need to maintain the kind of focus that kept him alive when enemy hornets were swarming him between the clouds. No more jokes about the Kaiser.

He caught a look at himself in a rainbow-colored pool of oily water. His cheeks were smooth but more haggard than he remembered them. What had become of the boy on the rope swing?

"All aboard," Roby said.

Alec climbed into the Marienfelde, doubting himself for the first time since he donned his uniform. They could not reach the Alps. Could they at least fly far enough to slip beyond the reach of this war and the men who maintained it?

He and Roby rode in silence to the city's edge and then into the countryside, where the road turned to dirt and rock. Crops were being grown everywhere a farmer could force a plow, in hopes of staving off food shortages come wintertime. Two men with leathery faces repaired a windmill in a field of malnourished cows.

And then they saw it.

The gargantuan anti-aircraft weapon stood on four steel wheels that were three times the diameter of the Marienfelde's tires. Those wheels were secured to the earth by brackets that had been hammered into the ground. Sandbags encircled racks of shells bigger than Alec's arm. The gun itself, mounted on what was essentially a flat deck connected to a pair of axles, featured a gunner's seat and a series of gears to dial in the proper elevation. The barrel was a broad pipe painted Prussian blue and aimed at the sky.

"Jesus," Alec whispered.

Men crawled over the gun like primates in uniform, inspecting the huge machine while they smoked and laughed. The spotter crew positioned nearby used a stereoscopic lens that looked like a pair of connected periscopes to take occasional glances to the west, where there was nothing to see.

"A real brute, isn't it?" Roby said.

"I've never seen one this close before."

"There's more."

Alec followed Roby's nod to see two small but vicious thirty-seven-millimeter machine guns fixed to improvised platforms that looked to be fashioned of welded automobile fenders. Each of these flaming onions sported five barrels. A two-man team could rip a plane in half from five thousand feet away.

Roby asked, "One bomb can take these three out?"

"If Ellenor times it correctly when we fly over, yes."

"And she can do that?"

"To tell you the truth, old boy, we've not yet even practiced."

Roby snorted and made the sign of the cross.

Alec did not share the man's misgivings. He did not doubt Ellenor. Why his belief in her was so resolute was a question that eluded him. The history they shared was brief, so that could not account for his trust in her. Instead, it was the opposite. The future they would share after tonight somehow retroactively cemented his faith. And that made not a bit of sense, least of all to Alec himself.

Twenty minutes later, they rumbled behind the trees where Hildegard waited.

Her disguise had held up. This far from the road leading to Metz, the strip of land between the trees was rarely visited. A thick line of oaks and flowering shrubs wrapped around the stretch of uninteresting ground where the Rumpler was concealed behind a blind of deadfall and piled leaves.

Alec and Roby got out of the truck and took their time sharing a cigarette while they waited to see if anyone had followed them. Minutes passed. No one appeared from the underbrush. Other than the birds, the world was quiet. Satisfied they were alone, they worked swiftly to fill the aircraft's primary tank as well as the auxiliary tank that was positioned in the gap behind the pilot's seat. Alec needed to give the bird a final inspection before they lifted off tonight, but it would have to wait. He still needed to train Ellenor in the function of the range finder and the lever that released the bombs.

He smoked the last of his cigarettes during the return drive to the city, with two hours to go before dusk.

****

At that same moment, not so very far away, a woman in soiled overalls and rolled-up shirtsleeves entered Café Lindsey. Gustov gazed at her with little interest until her eyes settled on him and her face hardened. She was here for him. He removed his boots from the table near the hearth and allowed the front legs of his chair to return to the floor. He'd been reading a state-issued pamphlet about the dangers of spilling secrets to prostitutes; it warned about pillow talk being used against good Germans by those dastardly Frogs. Gustov was pitying the poor writers tasked with producing this drivel when the woman approached him, grimy cap in her hands.

"Are you him?" she asked in lieu of an introduction.

Gustov had spent the last forty-five minutes dealing with angry policemen and signing various forms regarding the shooting. He sighed. "Am I *whom*?"

"Was told you had money for information."

"I might or might not. Several enterprising individuals have come forward this afternoon with similar hopes, but not one has produced any worthwhile intelligence. As I must soon depart, I am beginning to think that my efforts have been for naught. Is that the case with you?"

"I saw him."

"Of course you did." He set the pamphlet aside. On the cover was a lurid illustration of a woman whispering to a caricature of a French soldier. "Explain yourself, please."

"I work with scrap metal. Drive around. Collect what I can. Sell it to the government."

Gustov wasn't surprised. By necessity, women had taken on all manner of vocations traditionally held by men. Women were digging ditches and hand-pressing rifle cartridges from reclaimed brass. "A noble job that is a boon to us all," he said. "What else?"

"On my route I saw men buying fuel. They weren't military."

"So?"

"They were buying a lot of it, like the army does. I've never known civilians to get that much at once. Seen one of them around before, but the other I didn't recognize."

"Where did this transaction take place?"

She described a fuel yard used by the railroad and gave him the address.

"There was no woman with them?"

She shook her head.

Gustov pondered it. An anomalous fuel purchase didn't automatically implicate the Englander. But something about it—or perhaps in the way this rumpled messenger comported herself—told him it was worth investigating. Besides, it wasn't as if he had any other leads.

"Very well." He reached into his jacket and retrieved a packet of carefully folded *Deutsche Marks*. "I hope this is enough to make a difference." He tossed the money to the table and was on his feet and moving toward the door even before the woman had snatched it up.

With no vehicle at his disposal, he paid a chimney sweep with a motorized cart to ferry him halfway across the city, knowing that he either needed to leave within the hour or telegraph Mier to let him know he'd be late in returning. His investigation had been inefficient, which nettled him. Even worse, he'd earned the ire of the local law-enforcement authorities. They'd made it clear during their interview that a few of them wanted to arrest him for excessive use of force, even if they were ultimately overruled by their commanding officer. Gustov was working this town on borrowed time.

He spoke to the guard at the fuel facility's gate, but he was met with shrugs and vacant responses. By now he understood the currency of this beleaguered town and paid the sentry twice what he'd given the woman who'd sent him here. And that was the key that unlocked the guard's loyalties, such as they were. He'd seen the two men and described them both in detail. The blond hair and leather coat matched the description given by Father's stablemaster, Josef, when he'd told Gustov of the Englander with the bandaged hand.

Gustov felt like exhaling a great sound of relief, but he kept himself in check. His father had taught him, just as he'd been taught himself, to hold his emotions like he held his cards at the table. Nevertheless, excitement replaced frustration, and the fever of the hunt returned.

He'd been asking the same question all day, but now he selected a very different question, one to which he already knew the answer: "These men, did they purchase approximately two hundred and twenty liters?"

The guard frowned. "How do you know that?"

"Because that, my friend, is the amount of fuel required to fill a Rumpler C.IV."

"I don't know what that means."

Gustov swatted him cheerfully on the arm, spun around on his boot heel, and summoned his ride. His prey was nearby and apparently planning another flight. Gustov needed to return to the Fokker and get into the sky. Once there, he would simply circle and wait.

The Englander's next flight would be his last.

Part Three
The Dogfight

Chapter Twenty-Four

On what would be her last evening in Metz, and perhaps in Germany altogether, Ellenor suddenly realized the one thing she'd overlooked in her failed beehives. Leaning there against the cold stone wall of the free-shooters' subterranean lair, she thought about her *other* colonies, the good ones, the two that were alive and thriving. She'd been so proud of them. She'd harvested honey from them a few weeks ago and delivered a jar to everyone on Father's farm. Each time she opened the hive lid to inspect the frames, she found brood in various stages of development—from eggs to larvae to pupae—along with a healthy queen. The bees multiplied so quickly she feared they'd run out of space unless she added more supers to their hive.

Those strong bees had robbed the others.

Like invaders in search of plunder, the bees from the powerful colonies had raided the weak, absconding with honey and pollen alike. Though the defenders had done their best to ward off the assault, they were overwhelmed, their wax cells stripped of all treasures. With their warehouse empty, their delicate society collapsed. Those few bees that didn't starve likely departed in search of a new home.

"Having second thoughts about the plan?" Alec asked, misreading her expression.

Her bees had been robbed by their own kind. Was

there a lesson in that?

"Ellenor?"

She blinked. "Yes?"

"Doubting our endeavor?"

"Um... no more than is to be expected."

"We'll be fine."

"Can you promise me that?"

"You know I can't. If we allow even one of those ack-acks to get up and running before you and I are out of the way, we'll be in trouble, so we'll need to work fast. It won't be a stroll in a field of daisies, I can promise you that. I'm an optimist and a scofflaw but never a liar."

"You're certain I can learn what I need to know in such a short amount of time?"

"What's so difficult? You see the bad guys, you drop a bomb on their heads."

"I don't think it's going to be that easy."

"It won't be."

"I've never killed anyone. Or even *tried* to kill anyone, with the exception of you."

He grinned, flexing his fingers. "I've heard that women find scars to be attractive."

"I'm sure it was a man who first said that."

"No doubt. We're all so very insecure."

Ellenor was just about to explain her hypothesis about the honey thieves when Roby interrupted by handing her a bundle of clothing bound in twine. "You need something else to wear, and this was the best we could find, a WAAC uniform."

"Whack?"

He spelled it for her, then explained. "The Women's Auxiliary Army Corps provides support services to the British military. These were found in the suitcase of one of their administrators."

"And how did you come to possess this suitcase?"

He shook his head and didn't explain.

Ellenor assumed the garments' original owner, whoever she was, had been killed. It seemed appropriate: on the night Ellenor would attack the enemy, she would wear a dead woman's clothes.

She went upstairs to change. She found sufficient privacy in one of the former horse stalls, this one partially filled with buckets and trowels being used by the laborers who repaired the brick-faced streets. That done, she examined herself as best she could without the aid of a mirror. She wore a single-breasted khaki jacket with three buttons, fancy shoulder straps, and generous pockets. It was belted at the waistline. The buttons were leather, due to the universal metal shortage. Each shoulder strap was decorated with a badge shaped like a rose. The matching skirt was longer than she preferred, falling to only a foot from the ground. The outfit had come with a matching top and tie, but Ellenor eschewed them in favor of her black roll-neck wool sweater, now that it had finally been cleaned.

She pulled on her tall boots, which Uli had shined last night with polish as black as petroleum. Then she rejoined her companions in the catacombs just in time to catch Alec buttoning up a new shirt with a starched collar. He'd traded his worn trousers for a pair of whipcord breeches that fit him well. In a canvas tote beside him was a collection of coats, mufflers, and masks to keep them warm when the air grew thin.

Rolling his sleeves up to his forearms, Alec said

quietly so the others couldn't hear, "Would it be all right of me to say that you look nice?"

"My mother always told me to accept compliments but never take them too seriously."

"A wise woman. But still…"

She smiled. "Thank you." She gave nothing else away, but if truth were told, his words affected her to an unusual degree. She was scared about what was happening tonight, so everything was out of proportion, including the sudden blush in her cheeks.

"I asked Roby if he could find me a tuxedo," Alec said, "because I remember quite clearly that you accused all pilots of being…what was the phrase? *Rich little vandals.* So I was intending to dress appropriately."

"I'm sorry for saying that. I didn't know you."

"Actually, you were spot-on. Well, with the exception of the 'rich' part. But I've spent every moment since then trying to show you a better version of myself. So do I look serious and adult enough for you now?"

"I said I was sorry. And yes, you look very gentlemanly."

"That's too bad. I was hoping for *dashing.*"

Ellenor gave him a little roll of her eyes and realized they were flirting, which was something that hadn't happened to her in—

"Little brother," Sarah said, appearing at his side. "Do you have a moment?"

Alec let his eyes linger on Ellenor. He seemed about to say something—whatever it was, she was desperate to hear it—but he only nodded, turned away, and followed Sarah across the room.

Ellenor watched him go, wondering.

****

Alec glanced back at Ellenor, afraid he'd never recapture the moment. He admitted it to himself: she looked stunning in her uniform, her dark hair free over her shoulders. But then Sarah's voice forced him to pay attention to her. She had him sit on one of two empty onion crates she'd pulled to the far corner of the cellar.

He understood, then, that this might be the last time he spoke with his sister until the war was over. It crimped his heart.

She spoke before he could sort out his emotions. "I want your assurance that you're making the right decision with your choice of gunner."

"Gunner?"

"Is Ellenor the best option for this mission?"

Alec almost replied with something he would have regretted, but then he was struck by how much he adored this woman who had been a girl just the other day. "I've missed you."

She softened; only Alec could do that to her so easily. "Me, too. I'm sorry it's worked out this way."

"It's not over yet."

"You were always the more optimistic half of us."

"And you were the realist."

"Still am. Hence my question."

Alec sighed. "She will be fine. I'll show her. Besides, as soon as that last bomb drops, I'm banking my wings and getting the hell out of here. I wouldn't have time to land and swap out Roby for Ellenor before the German response arrived. It has to be this way."

"Now who's the realist? But I think you may have ulterior motives. You have no intention of letting that girl out of your sight."

"I think she'd prefer the term *woman*, and you're right. You see right through me, which is not newsworthy in the least, since it's been happening for decades. The idea of flying away with her sounds...well, it sounds like more than I deserve."

"Have you told her as much?"

"Good God, sis, I'm as brave as the next chap, but my courage has its limits."

"Coward. Now let me change the subject. The clock is moving."

Alec motioned for her to proceed.

"When the bells at Basilique Saint-Vincent sound at midnight, Roby, Jules, and I will light the fires. If everything works as we're expecting, it will require at least twenty minutes to flood the bunker with smoke. We've scouted the windows, vents, and exits. We know what to do. But it might take as long as half an hour. Do you still have Daddy's pocket watch?"

"No. It was in my kit when I crashed five days ago. I never went back for it."

"Jules has one he'll give to you. It's an inexpensive model, but it tells the time. So at half past midnight, you get that plane off the ground and blow those goddamn guns to pieces."

Alec had no questions about this blunt-edged plot that Sarah had devised. He suspected that, at least in some small way, she was using him to further her own misguided agenda. But he didn't care. It didn't change what he felt for her. "What will you do after tonight?" he asked her quietly.

"I suppose I'll start by speaking with Klaus. I promised Ellenor that I would. She was right when she said he deserved to know."

"Can you trust him?"

"He means well. I can't say anything more than that."

"You won't be able hide down here forever. Where will you go?"

"Maybe to the country. Stefan had a small cottage. I suppose it's mine now. He talked about wanting to spend time there and write a novel or something literary and foolish like that."

"What about going to France?"

"I don't know anyone in France, little brother. You want me to be safe, but as long as this war goes on, there's nowhere that qualifies. The Ottomans are fighting us in North Africa. Belgium's a disaster. The Zeppelins are bombing London, so even home isn't safe."

"It's a big planet, from what I hear. Surely there's somewhere…"

She gave him a tight smile. "I should be asking you the same question. Where will *you* go? After you drop that last bomb, you'll need to choose a destination and choose it quickly. As you said, even if we succeed in flushing out the telegraph team, it won't take them long to regroup and call for help."

"Hildegard has a considerable range. We can make it a long way."

"Listen to you, using a plural pronoun."

"What's that supposed to mean?"

"You know what it means. I see you sitting here in front of me. But part of you is across the room with her."

Alec shook his head when he felt the warmth in his

face. No one but Sarah could get to him like that.

"Tell me it's not true," she said.

"What can I say? Happens to the best of us sooner or later."

"Would you like my blessing?"

"Do I need it?"

She touched him on the arm. There was a time when the two of them were inseparable, and only after her hand made contact with him did he realize how many years had passed since the days of their antics, their carefree songs. "You've always needed it. And I've needed yours. You gave me permission to come here to Germany, where I found a life and friends I admire. My place is still here. I can do good things. But you have something else waiting for you. Take her and find it."

"That sounds suspiciously like the beginning of one of the stories you used to tell me when we were children."

"And didn't those stories always have happy endings?"

He put his hand on hers. "I will see you again, Sarah Corbin-Dawes of Derby."

"You will. And we'll celebrate a free Europe."

He was just about to say something else—anything to make the moment last—but she swept him into a hug, which he returned with intensity. They held on.

Roby's voice ended their embrace: "It's time."

Alec followed Sarah to where the others had gathered around the city map and hand-drawn diagrams. The electrical current that crawled up his spine was the very same one that he felt at the aerodrome each time the captain outlined the next

216

mission. Objectives were important. Tactics were important. But woven through all of that was an element of prodigious risk, the cold probability that someone on the team would not make it back. Alec had earned the title of ace because he thrived in that environment, even though his teeth rattled during combat and his balls felt packed in ice.

"This is how it will happen," Sarah said.

Everyone waited and watched.

"Roby will drive Alec and Ellenor to their plane, along with the supplies readied for them. Roby will then return here, where he and Jules and I will pack and compress the burnables. We'll make more than we need, just in case. At one hour before midnight, we'll leave, arriving at the bunker approximately twenty minutes later." She used a screwdriver as a pointer. "Here and here are the two most obvious entry points for the smoke, and also these smaller windows here and here. At exactly midnight, we'll light the burnables, smash the glass, and place them inside. If we've done our jobs correctly, they'll burn slowly and produce an abundance of smoke. The only thing that can go wrong at this point is if we're spotted by someone before we're finished."

"And if we are?" Roby asked.

"We'll be armed. We'll do what we have to do."

Roby nodded solemnly.

"The bunker's interior is approximately two hundred square meters. Thank God it's not a very large space."

"Wait," Alec said. "Aren't the windows fortified somehow? What if you can't get your fire inside the building?"

"The windows are highly secure because they're narrow. They're like arrow slits in an old castle. No full-grown adult could wiggle through one of those unless he happened to be a carnival contortionist. But the oil-soaked bundles we've made are sized to fit."

"Glad to hear it."

"We tested one of them earlier outside of town. It produced so much smoke that we're anticipating the radio operators inside will abandon ship in a matter of minutes. At half past midnight, Alec and Ellenor will get in the air and do the rest."

"What about contingencies if something goes wrong?" Alec asked. "What about backup plans?"

"There are none."

"Well, that's comforting. And here I was beginning to worry."

"If the smoke doesn't work, or if we get intercepted before we can deliver it, then you two are on your own. The German planes from airfields in nearby towns will be alerted within minutes."

Ellenor crossed her arms in a posture of concern. "Can we outrun them?"

"There's no moon tonight," Alec said. "We won't be faster than they are, but Hildegard can climb to twenty thousand feet. It will be dark. They'll never see us."

"How cold is it at twenty thousand feet?" she asked.

"Oh, I'd say a balmy fifteen degrees below zero or so, but the wind makes it feel about fifty degrees colder."

"People actually fly that high?"

"Believe it or not."

"They'd freeze to death, wouldn't they?"

"When I was an observer on a high-altitude run, they made me wear an insulated suit with so many layers that I had to be hoisted into my seat by a team of mechanics. I could barely move to work the camera, let alone the gun. I hear these days they're experimenting with electrically heated trousers. Not sure how I feel about that."

Sarah got them back on track. "We've given you all the extra clothing we can spare. That will have to be enough. Now, shortly after that first detonation, the city sirens will be activated, and all of Metz will go into bombing protocol. Every unnecessary light will be extinguished. Shutters will be closed. That will make it all the more difficult for you to see well enough to score a direct hit on the rest of your targets. Are you prepared for that?"

"We will be," Alec assured her.

"Are you sure? That same darkness that will keep you safe will also work against you."

"I said we'll be fine. We won't miss our targets. I have something in mind."

"Would you care to share?"

"I know you trust me, sis. Me and no one else."

She paused for a moment, then said, "One of these days, that trust in you will likely be my undoing."

He grinned like he was twelve years old and had just tied a rocket to her bicycle seat.

Then Sarah did something Alec had not predicted at all: she stepped around the table and pulled him close. "I love you, little brother."

"I love you back."

"We can do this, right?"

He withdrew just enough to give her his most formidable and reassuring smile, though he did not feel formidable nor assured in the least. "Consider it done."

Chapter Twenty-Five

In the burnished light of late afternoon, on the same day he'd killed an unruly civilian, Gustov prepared his triplane for whatever the coming night held in store. The aircraft's nose and three wing decks were painted a color the Voss family genealogist called *jacinth orange*, named after a gemstone embedded in the pommel of the swept-hilt rapier hanging in the library of Gustov's paternal grandfather.

The mechanic he'd conscripted from the local airfield sat on an overturned bucket and looked nervous. Gustov would need him when the time came to fire the Fokker's engine.

He checked his wristwatch; he was the only man in his squadron who owned one. Then he took a seat on the lower wing deck and swung his legs back and forth, searching for a tune to whistle but finding nothing to his liking.

Even if the Englander was miles from the city when he lifted off in the Rumpler, his engine noise would give him away. Gustov looked to the sky and waited for the man to appear.

****

Alec and Ellenor watched Roby's lorry disappear through the trees.

Alec said, "It's only us now."

"I'm sorry about Sarah. I wish you didn't have to

be apart from her."

"It's not your fault."

"Isn't it?"

He felt her nearness. She stood beside him, no more than two inches away. "Don't be silly," he told her. "None of it is anyone's fault, except maybe God's."

"You shouldn't say such things. Some would call it sacrilege."

"Bugger that. Any god who abides trench warfare isn't worthy of the name."

"You think He should intervene?"

"I don't know what I think. I just want a well-mixed drink on a warm veranda and no barbed wire in sight."

She turned and looked up at him. "Where is this veranda of yours located?"

"Where would you like it to be?"

"Don't ask questions like that if you don't mean it."

"I completely mean it." He startled himself by saying that. It just came out. Now, with her eyes on him, he groped around for a follow-up line but didn't find much. "What I'm saying is…I'm glad you're going with me, that we're going together."

"Me, too. But…where?"

"I'm still working on that."

"You better work faster."

"Sarah said that nowhere is safe. I'm hoping she isn't right." He glanced at the sun, which was a few notches closer to the western horizon than it had been moments before. "I should, uh, give Hildegard one last inspection."

"Of course."

Alec, holding back all manner of inconvenient emotions, stepped away and gave as much of his attention as possible to the plane. He knelt and inspected the explosives array. Each of the four bombs weighed fifty pounds and was painted a rather pleasant sky blue—an odd aesthetic choice for a weapon of such destructive power. From extensive briefings on enemy armaments, he knew these were designed by the German Air Service's experimental workshop, *Prüfanstalt und Werft*. These four PuWs were activated by a nose fuse that ignited upon impact. The TNT crammed into these solid steel meteorites wouldn't eradicate all of the anti-aircraft guns, but it would destroy enough to clear a path for the French flyers, assuming Ellenor hit all of her targets.

"Is everything all right?" she asked, crouching beside him.

"So far."

She pointed to a length of wire extruding from Hildegard's navel. "What is that?"

"It's an aerial for the wireless Morse unit. I believe you Yanks call it an 'antenna.'"

"I see. I wish we could use the wireless to call for help."

"Who would we call?"

"Woodrow Wilson."

"The American president? And what on earth would we say to him?"

"Oh, I don't know. Dear Mr. Wilson. We've gotten ourselves into a tight spot. We need to wipe out a lot of guns so that our allies can in turn wipe out a factory. Please send the Marines and chocolate."

"Chocolate?"

"It's my fantasy. If you don't like it, you can get your own."

He laughed. "I like it just fine. Chocolate it is, then. But…it's okay to be nervous."

"Thanks. Is it that obvious?"

"It's fine. Come on. I need to teach you the controls before it's too dark to see." He took her hand, helping her onto the wing near the observer's seat and feeling the warmth of her touch spread up his arm. He let go before it burned him, then quickly got on with the lesson. He gestured to a contraption that resembled a microscope, mounted near her seat. "This device is how you'll track your targets. All pilots begin as observers when we're training, so I've had my wicked way with these spotting scopes, or at least the kind made in Britain. I'm assuming this model functions the same way. Basically, it works by taking a reading with this attached stopwatch on a fixed object on the ground. You use that as a benchmark. Once you're doing it for real, you refer back to your previous readings, make adjustments for altitude and speed, and then wait for the target to cross the calculated point in your sight. At that precise moment, you release the first bomb using this control lever here, which pulls a cable that is wired to the egg basket, and Bob's your uncle."

Ellenor stared at him blankly.

"Right-o. Now, let's do the math on a sample flight. Say we're at four thousand feet and advancing at three-quarter speed dead into the wind to eliminate drift, and we—"

"Stop."

"Yes?"

"Please tell me you're kidding."

He smiled, having barely been able to hold it in. "I am. Actually, the plan is to forget this sighting mechanism and fly only a hundred feet from the ground so you can slip the bombs right into their hip pockets."

She swatted him on the arm. "This is serious."

"Is it?"

"Men will die tonight. I will kill them, *me*. I can think of nothing more serious than that."

"You won't kill anyone. The ack-ack crews will be called to their guns only if they're alerted of incoming enemy aircraft. They don't just sit around their cannons trading tobacco rations when there's nothing to do. I doubt anyone will be posted there when we make our surprise appearance."

"How can you be sure?"

"What other option do we have, El? Let our French cousins get slaughtered when the raid arrives tomorrow morning?" In way of empathy, he tried to remember his first time on a combat assignment, his virgin outing, but the images intersected in ways that made no sense. Each time he faced off against a man in another plane, he accepted his own death, and that acceptance muddled his memory. "It's not going to be easy. But I got you into this sordid ordeal, and I'll damn sure do everything in my power to get you to the other side."

"And where is this other side?"

"I told you I'm working on it. Hildegard has a range of at least three hundred miles, depending on the direction of the wind, which gives us some options."

"Options for what?"

"For where we'll go next. Honestly, I've no idea where we'll be this time tomorrow, how we'll sleep, what we'll eat. I'm just trying to get us through the next few hours. I ruined your life, so the least I can do is give you a shot at another one."

Her gaze was soft. "My life isn't ruined."

"Yes, well, give me time, and I'm sure I'll get around to it." The pressure of her eyes made him more nervous than he ever was in combat. He tried to sidestep it by pointing at the machine gun mounted on the swivel track that encircled Ellenor's seat. "Don't worry about the Parabellum here. I don't anticipate that you'll be peeling off any bullets at the ack-acks, but if this gun is in your way so you can't see when you're releasing the bombs, you can unlock it right here and simply slide it around the ring. Got it?" He showed her how it was done.

"I think so."

"Sarah is worried that we can't hit our targets in the dark. My solution, which I wisely did not tell her, is that we fly so low to the ground that we can't miss."

"Flying low sounds very dangerous."

"To some, perhaps. I'm shitty at most things, El, but on the average day I'm an above-average pilot, and on certain rare days I too am quite rare." At that moment, the sun melted into the sky's edge. Alec consulted the pocket watch Sarah had given him. He could barely see its face. "It's almost eight-thirty. We should get our things ready."

"We have four hours to wait."

"What would you have us do, then? Sit and watch the stars?"

"Does that sound so terrible? I realize that we're not normal people, but normal people do that kind of thing to pass the time. Besides, if I don't stop thinking about what's coming at midnight, I'm going to be sick. So unless you want me vomiting all over this plane—"

"Say no more." He jumped from the wing and helped her down. Before she could utter another word, he retrieved Magnild's quilt and unfurled it in a choice location near the fuselage, creating an amphitheater of sorts from which they could count the constellations. Feeling athletic and loose like he always did when a flight was imminent, he dropped onto the blanket, extended his legs, and leaned back on his hands. Then he held his breath.

After a few moments, Ellenor sat down beside him.

Alec exhaled, pretending to study the stars.

****

On the advice of a dandelion, Ellenor Jantz had come to Germany in search of adventure. The wish she'd made back then had unfolded as all wishes do— in ways we cannot anticipate, in moments we can't foresee. Despite the fear of settling into the observer's seat and making herself a part of the violence she abhorred, she would enter that dark place when it was time and trust she'd find her way out. It would be the scariest thing she'd ever done.

"I don't have a penny," Alec said, sitting beside her on the quilt.

"I'm sorry?"

"For your thoughts. I'd offer you one, but I'm afraid I'm rather destitute."

"So am I." She knew exactly the amount of money she'd saved in the little cedar coffer in her room at Father's house. She could not return there without being arrested by the airmen who occupied the property. Her money had probably already been confiscated, along with her clothing, her books, and her tortoiseshell brush. "I hope they leave the hives alone."

"What will happen to the bees with you no longer tending them?"

"If no one disturbs them, they'll do what they do best, turning nectar into honey and using it to get through the winter. They don't need my help for that. And when they outgrow their hive next spring, they'll find somewhere new."

"You mean like us?"

"I suppose so...assuming you've decided on somewhere for us to go."

"Do you like surprises?"

"Is that your way of admitting that you still haven't found a suitable destination?"

"There's a lot to be said for spontaneity. But the breeze is blowing from the northwest, which will naturally nudge Hildegard to the southeast. Hopefully there's something in that direction that isn't being torn to pieces by the war."

Ellenor tried to summon a mental map of Europe but found it difficult to concentrate. She knew Italy was down there somewhere, but it sounded awfully far away. The only things that made sense were the *near* things, the things she could reach and shape and bend to her will.

"We'll just fly until we see that veranda," Alec said. "Then we can toast to our success and to Sarah's good health, and we'll sing pub songs all night until we collapse."

"I don't know any pub songs. I'll just hum along in the background."

"Nonsense. I'll teach you."

"I look forward to it."

"No reason to wait." He kept his gaze skyward but tilted his head as if sorting through a catalog of bawdy tunes.

"If you're thinking of serenading me, then this is probably not the best time…"

And then Alec began to sing.

Beside a German shell hole, when the smoke had cleared away,

beneath a busted Camel, its former pilot lay;

his throat was cut by the bracing wire, the tank had hit his head,

and, coughing out his dental work, these parting words he said:

"Oh, I'm going to a better land—they binge there every night;

the cocktails grow on bushes, so everyone stays tight;

they've torn up all the calendars, they've busted all the clocks,

and little drops of whiskey come trickling down the rocks."

Alec's voice gained strength, carrying into the darkness.

The pilot breathed these last few gasps before he passed away:

"I'll tell you how it happened. My rudders didn't stay.

The motor wouldn't hit at all, the struts were far too few,

A shot went through the petrol tank and let it all leak through.

Oh, I'm going to a better land where the motors

always run,

Where guns don't jam and airplane wings don't melt before the sun.

They've got no Sops, they've got no Spads, they've got no DH.4s,

and little frosted juleps are served at all the stores."

Ellenor laughed without reservation, clapping half a dozen times. "Bravo!"

Alec dipped his head in a little bow and looked pleased with her reaction.

"You, sir, are full of surprises."

"You should see me when I'm one hundred percent." He held up his patched-up hand. "Give me a few days, and I'll show you my penchant for ballads on an Irish fiddle."

Before she could rein herself in, Ellenor gave in to the candor of the moment and carefully took his hand. "May I?"

He nodded slowly.

Ellenor loosened the white cotton strip and uncoiled it. Alec watched her. She could make out no details now that the night had fully settled around them, but she traced the contours of the wound with her fingertip. "You caught the bullet."

"Knocked it out of the way, really."

"Impressive, nonetheless."

"In my line of work, reflexes are worth more than money or morality."

She completed her finger's journey around his injury. "Does it still hurt?"

"A little. Let's see if we can do something about that." He closed his hand around hers. Then he took the bandage she'd removed and slowly wrapped it around their joined fingers. She stared at him as he did it, binding the fabric so that their palms were pressed together, one layer of white cotton on top of the next. Her hand was tight against his. Then he tucked the end of the bandage into itself and said, "That's better."

When Ellenor was fifteen, she'd witnessed her first snow in New Mexico. Her papa had taken the family by train to visit relatives in the Sangre de Cristo Mountains. The flakes had dazzled her, silvery-white in the sun, tingling her bare arms as she raised her hands to the sky. Looking upward into that falling snow was like moving through the stars. Nothing had truly taken her breath away since then—until now.

"Everywhere I fly from this point on," Alec said, "I fly with you."

She wanted the same, wanted it in a way that made no sense. Leaning into him, she used her free hand to find his face. He used his to capture her hair behind her head, bringing her even closer. Their foreheads touched. They remained like that for a long time, sharing warmth and anticipation. Ellenor's breath came so lightly that she felt weightless; only their bound fists anchored them and kept her from floating away.

He kissed her.

She pushed her mouth hard against his. All of her joy and longing was contained in that kiss, and so too was her sadness and fear. Everything she'd lost and everything she stood to gain was pushed into him as she exhaled. When she took a breath, she drew him in. He tasted like whiskey and smoke and the cherry candies they'd shared in Roby's truck.

She fell back onto the quilt, and with her hand still

bound to his, pulled him on top of her.

Though binding their hands together had seemed devoutly romantic a moment ago, now it impeded Alec in his attempts to divest himself of his trousers and her of her skirt. She assisted him. Working together—and giggling occasionally—they managed to rid themselves of just enough clothing that their bare skin touched in a way that made Ellenor cast away what little trepidation remained. She locked her legs around him and made a predatory sound when he ran his tongue up her neck.

She reached between her legs and pulled him inside of her.

The two of them moved in perfect synchronization, as if they'd never be separated. The stars high above looked on with cold indifference, knowing that nothing—not even starlight—was forever.

Chapter Twenty-Six

Alec dreamed of bones in the mud. He ran bent at the waist through a trench so filled with water and piss that every stride was a struggle. His rifle was frozen to his hands, the tips of his fingers purple with frostbite, like hardened grapes. Exploding shells blew dirt cascades across the lip of the trench, where bloated bodies floated in the muck. And wildly overhead, untouched by it all, flew a single, soaring plane, its pilot an angel with muslin wings.

"Alec, listen."

He opened his eyes instantly, the dream vanishing. He saw the night sky framing Ellenor's face, her hair loose. "You're beautiful," he told her.

"Kind of you to say, but the bells are ringing."

The distant chimes of Basilique Saint-Vincent carried across the darkness.

She kissed him. "It's time."

He got dressed without speaking. At some point they had untied their joined hands. Alec saw it all over again, her rolling on top of him, her black sweater pulled over her head and cast away—

The dream returned. Men drowned in their own goddamned trench. He could have been one of them, a member of the infantry, where human life seemed to have no value. Perhaps he *should* have been. Only luck and reflexes had saved him.

As he pulled on his shirt, he bumped against her. He turned, barely able to see her but sensing the awkwardness their silence had created. In an effort to dispel it, he said, "When you meet my mother one day, it will be best not to mention this part."

"If I meet your mother, I'm telling her everything."

He smiled to himself. They were going to be fine.

Alec pulled on his boots. Behind him, Ellenor did the same.

As mighty as Hildegard might have been, her petrol tanks were insufficient to fly all the way from here to the Channel and then to England. Alec loved the idea of returning with Ellenor on his arm, the prettiest woman in all of Derbyshire. The two of them could settle into the sedate business of news printing and attend Saturday evening socials at the civic hall.

It sounded dreadful. Boring and dreadful. And that northwesterly wind had other ideas.

Once dressed, he helped her to her feet. Before she could say another word, he pulled her close, resting his chin on her head and breathing the perfume of her hair. Every flight was dangerous, this more than most. They'd be moving at a hazardously low altitude in full darkness, so close to the ground that any German with a sidearm was a threat. If one of those flaming onions managed to let loose, they were finished. Even though Ellenor would be seated directly behind him, there was a solid chance he'd never speak to her again.

He knew she understood this. He felt it in her embrace.

The cathedral bells had stopped ringing. At this very moment, Sarah and her friends were shoving burning bundles into windows.

"You've got to pull the propeller now," he said.

"Lucky for me I'm an expert."

He was afraid to release her. "Listen, whatever happens to us tonight—"

She put her fingers over his lips. "Tell me everything when we land."

That was all she needed to say. Alec didn't necessarily share her faith in the outcome, but that turbulent energy was back in his blood, the borderline madness that always gripped him before a flight. Win or lose, live or die, he would do it with his teeth bared to the wind. "You ready for this?"

By way of response, she put on her pith helmet and tightened the strap below her chin.

He smiled, infatuated with her courage, and then pulled himself into the plane.

****

Propeller churning, wheels thumping, tail skid plowing a furrow in the field, the aircraft built speed as Ellenor hooked the safety belt across her lap. The goggles they'd given her dangled at her neck, and she hurriedly got them fixed over her eyes as the breeze in her face became a gale. Each rut the wheels encountered sent a jolt through her wooden stool and all the way up her spine. She clamped her teeth together. Directly in front of her, Alec's scarf fluttered like a flag.

Then everything changed. The plane ceased contact with the ground. The banging and heaving were replaced with an exhilarating pressure that forced her into her seat; the fight against gravity had commenced. Tilted backward, she watched the yawning night sky spread wide and vast before her. For a few moments, the plane almost seemed to stall, caught in a defiance of physics. Then, by brute determination, it muscled its way higher and leveled off.

Alec swung them toward Metz.

Ellenor took the first of what would be hundreds of glances over the side of the plane, first the left and then the right, trying to get her bearings. The land below lay in shadow. By touch she located the lever that was hitched to the release cable. Having found it, she let go, afraid of yanking it by accident and vaporizing a city block. Metz appeared, a glimmer of tiny lights from lamps and fires and gas-powered bulbs along the streets.

She reminded herself to breathe deliberately, one after the next.

Alec lowered them closer to the ground. They skimmed the treetops and rushed toward the city's defenses at sixty, then seventy miles an hour. Nothing earthbound could match these speeds.

Alec dipped the nose slightly. He held up his right hand in a signal that appeared in silhouette against the sky. He pointed down repeatedly.

Ellenor saw the first anti-aircraft gun, its long tube pointed up, a single lantern at its base. It was fifty yards away, thirty yards away, twenty—

Frantically she grabbed the lever, looked over the side—

The plane passed over the target and left it behind. Alec threw up a hand in agitation.

Damn it! Ellenor looked back, but she was too late.

Alec banked them into a hard turn, slamming her against the fuselage's interior. She gave a sharp bark of pain. They were coming back around for another pass.

She could not miss again.

The plane leveled out, engine howling. Ellenor could barely make sense of her environment, with the darkness and unbelievable velocity, much less be expected to get her timing correct. But she had to try. She leaned over the side again, and this time when Alec gestured madly at the ground, she was ready. Her eyes focused on the only shape in an otherwise empty expanse. The plane charged toward it, devouring the distance.

"Three…two…"

She pulled the lever.

For the longest time, nothing happened. The plane sped toward its next target, the wind and the propeller too loud to ignore. But then a light appeared behind them, followed by the shockwave, followed by the sound. The ground behind them turned into a lake of fire.

Alec shouted something that Ellenor hoped was his approval. Too stunned to respond, she shoved the lever back into place, readying the next bomb. Had she actually done it? Her body buzzed so violently her teeth ached.

Alec held up two fingers, then tipped the right wings up and the left wings down, angling them toward the second of their four targets…

Something flew directly in front of them.

Alec jerked the plane off course to avoid a collision, tossing Ellenor hard against her restraining belt. The force of the impact caused her to bite her tongue. She had no idea what was happening, or why. He'd warned her of the shrapnel bursts if one of those big guns was allowed to open fire, but this was a different thing. This had wings.

A German aircraft had found them.

****

Gustov had nearly given up when the sound of the distant engine shook him to his senses. He assumed that he'd misjudged the distance the fuel would be delivered, and the Rumpler was at least a hundred kilometers away. Or the Englander was nearby but had no intention of flying tonight. Either way, Gustov had rolled the dice and lost. He slumped in the plane's single seat with his head reclining on his rolled coat, hoping that Mier had brought all the boys home from the day's patrols. He'd rejoin them tomorrow.

Then a distinctive cry carried across the void.

He sat up. Held very still. Listened.

The aircraft's engine was far away but coming closer.

Gustov shouted at his borrowed mechanic, who'd fallen asleep in the summer grass. Even before the idiot had gotten to his feet, Gustov ran through his pre-flight check and struggled into his coat. The mechanic pulled the chocks as Gustov donned his goggles and padded cap. He squeezed his hands into his form-fitting gloves and yelled for the mechanic to engage the prop.

The Fokker lit up immediately. Gustov opened the throttle, rumbled across the field, and lifted into the air, gathering altitude as quickly as he could without stalling the engine. He was already several crucial minutes behind the Englander, wherever the man was going. The two planes boasted nearly equal top speeds, which meant Gustov would need to rely on wits and raw luck to close the gap.

As it turned out, there was no gap.

Gustov could be sure of nothing in the dark. The Rumpler was practically invisible. But for just a few seconds he caught sight of it framed against Metz's lamps below, and it seemed to be turning, following the outline of the city.

A second later, a firebomb appeared.

The explosion startled him so much he nearly swore. The night lit up with flames.

What the hell?

The Englander was bombing Metz.

Gustov kicked the rudder bar hard and dove after the man, cocking his guns as he went.

****

Alec searched frantically for the other plane. He'd avoided a collision by fortune more than skill, the two birds unable to see each other until it was nearly too late. The German response had been almost instantaneous. How had the bastard gotten into the air so quickly?

He looped Hildegard in wide spirals so as not to create a predictable line. She responded beautifully, graceful even though she weighed over one ton. She bobbed and darted hungrily at the slightest touch of her control wheel. It was like riding a shark through the sea.

Alec pointed her at the next ground target. He had to trust that his pursuer didn't know his destination and would be flying randomly in the dark. Alec had barely gotten a look at the enemy's craft; he knew it was a fighter—but what was it? A rickety old training model kept on hand for emergencies? Or something truly deadly? The thing's belly had flashed in front of Hildegard's prop too fast to reveal more.

The ice moved like medicine through Alec's veins.

Everything felt cold, a sensation that had kept him alive for over a year as a pilot because it numbed his pulse and calmed his breathing. Many times it had turned him into a killer. He guided Hildegard over the rooftops and belfries of Metz, wheels only a few feet from chimneys, turning his head in a constant search of the black sky.

The second ack-ack appeared.

Though the 90-millimeter gun was no more than a gray finger pointing upward, Alec's keen eyes recognized it. Keeping his left hand on the wheel, he waved his right in the air and then pointed like he was stabbing someone, hoping Ellenor was paying attention. They had to destroy these remaining weapons and then get the hell out of here before the German flyer made sense of the dark.

Alec turned his head: "*Do it! Do it now!*"

****

Gustov couldn't see for shit.

He'd almost rammed into the stolen Rumpler accidentally, narrowly missing, and now he'd lost the damn thing entirely. Fate had deigned to sentence him to a duel on a moonless night, so the only things he saw were the twinkle of innocent windows in the city below. A fire raged to the south.

Gustov went high.

The triplane ascended faster than any other bus he'd ever flown. It could climb to a thousand meters in only three minutes. Gustov didn't need that much height; he needed only to get above his enemy. Once there, he would be able to see the Rumpler framed against the glow of Metz, and then he would fall like a falcon, talons bared.

****

By the time Alec shouted—"*Do it! Do it now!*"—Ellenor had already pulled the lever. The bomb dropped. She'd been ready, barely able to breathe for the knot in the back of her throat. A direct hit wasn't necessary, as the explosion's radius would raze everything in the area.

She closed her eyes.

The noise ripped the night apart, sending steel and rocks in every direction. The plane wobbled as the force caught up with it. Ellenor's stomach swam.

She put her head over the side just in time to vomit into the air.

With no time to recover, she swallowed the gunk in her mouth and tried to focus, but a German in a plane was out there somewhere, hunting them. At any moment, she expected his guns to open up and shred her where she sat. What if the fuel tank caught fire and she burned to death? What if Alec were hit first, torn from her hours after he'd whispered his affections in her ear?

Bashert, Josef said in her mind: *destiny*.

"No, thanks," she replied. She spit the foul taste from her teeth and grabbed the lever.

****

Alec was not flying The Dragon. Had he been screwed into the seat of his cherished S.E.5, oh, how he would have enjoyed this joust. Hildegard wasn't as lithe, but she was strong, and Alec depended on that strength as he bent her into such a steep left turn that she stood nearly completely on her side in the air, her wings almost vertical, her struts straining, her wires keening.

Two anti-aircraft guns remained.

Alec leveled the plane, his head sweeping left to right in search of his foe. The German, whoever he was, had vanished. Alec needed to reach the other two targets before the Hun got a fix on them. He asked Hildegard for more speed, and she replied.

His strategy of flying low had so far succeeded. No doubt the people in the cramped houses below were thinking it a raid. Lights faded as lamps were extinguished. Alarms were probably being sounded and children were being whisked under dining tables to protect them, even though Alec had no intention of harming anyone but the AA crew. He'd studied Sarah's map and stenciled the position of the guns in his memory. He didn't need to be able to see them to understand the geometry of their destruction. Hildegard roared closer.

Alec didn't realize he was smiling.

****

From high above, Gustov saw his opponent. That was the first step in killing him.

The second step was getting within range and pouring bullets into him. Without thinking about it, he gave the guns the customary check, just to make sure they'd fire; sometimes the whole rig failed. But a slight squeeze of the trigger mechanism discharged a trio of tracer rounds into the clouds. Satisfied, Gustov reduced speed, angled the nose down, and drove the Fokker into a precipitous dive. He held the stick in both hands, cradling it between his legs, his gaze locked on the Rumpler that was outlined perfectly against the city below.

It occurred to him that he was about to fire on a German-built plane above a German-inhabited town. Of all the unlikely situations in which he'd found himself since his exploits as an airman began, this was the most radical: gun down a madman and his female partner who'd pilfered a plane in order to bomb a contested city. That sounded like a plot concocted by boys pretending to be pilots, their plane made of a crate on wheels borrowed from their little sister's pram.

He shoved the image away and dove toward his enemy's head.

****

Ellenor gripped the lever so hard the muscles pulsed painfully in her forearm. Her other hand, which had been tied to Alec's not very long ago, clutched the front of her coat so as to reduce the trembling. She sucked in cold wind, exhaling through her mouth in ragged little grunts. Five days ago, the most daring thing she'd ever done was inspect her hive frames without wearing gloves or a veil, risking a sting. And she'd thought herself brave. Jesus.

The plane streaked toward the next collection of guns, a cluster of armaments aimed upward, awaiting deployment. Men rushed toward them, soldiers intent on counterattacking. Now that they'd had time to respond, they charged their equipment. As the plane neared, the men gripped handles, threw off safety locks, and swiveled barrels. If even one of them acquired a target and opened fire, Ellenor and Alec would be much too close to the ground to evade the incoming rounds.

Alec must have realized the same thing, because he increased their speed. Ellenor could hardly breathe in the wind. How could anything manufactured by human hands move so fast? It was like being shackled to a storm.

Three, two—

By now she understood the pattern even if she couldn't explain the physics behind it.

—one.

The fireball murdered the gunners below. This time, Ellenor didn't close her eyes.

****

Bullets tore through Hildegard's wing.

Alec swore and banked right, jamming his foot on the rudder bar. Red streaks sliced the air, bullets coated with pyrotechnic gel streaming from the German's machine guns. Loose fabric fluttered around the half-dozen holes. Alec looked up in time to see the black, cross-like shape of the airplane above him. Seconds later, the German dropped directly behind them.

Alec almost panicked. He had almost panicked many times when locked in aerial warfare. It was part of the ritual. You went balls first against terror but never crossed its line, giving it the finger as you held fast to your wits. With the calm of a monk, Alec began evasive maneuvers, swinging first left and then dipping slightly and bringing his bird around in a rapid right-hand curve.

The German followed him and fired again.

Alec jiggled Hildegard instinctively, taking the rounds in the tail. The bullets thudded into the wood like fists against a barn door.

"*Alec!*"

He heard Ellenor's scream but could do nothing about it. The German behind him was a sorcerer, clinging fast despite Alec's efforts to elude him.

The fourth and final ack-ack battery, flanked by thirty-seven-millimeter flaming onions, waited only a quarter-mile ahead. If Alec was going to be beaten tonight by the German pilot, he would do his best to take those guns with him and clear a path for the French.

But he didn't want to lose the girl of his dreams. A heroic death sounded far less appealing than seeing her naked again.

He laughed and pushed Hildegard even closer to the ground.

****

"He's insane," Gustov said when the Englander dropped another ten meters. Soaring over the city, the two planes were so near the slanted rooftops that the Fokker's wheels nearly scraped the lip of a fireplace flue. Telegraph poles became crucifixes upon which he'd impale himself if he weren't careful. He worked the stick constantly, hypnotically, making tiny little adjustments that flicked his three wing decks just enough to keep him clear of the obstacles. The Rumpler, twice as large, had somehow tucked itself into a clear channel and moved like a slipstream between the centuries-old buildings.

A hundred meters back, Gustov fired.

Tracers squirted out as if from a hose, some of them swatting the Rumpler's right wing, some of them drilling into a house nearby. Each of his two guns was fed by a five-hundred-round ammunition drum. Always miserly with his ammo, he'd used only ten percent so far, hitting the Rumpler with at least three bursts. None of those, however, had struck anywhere near the fuel supply, the engine, or the pilot. The aircraft was so well engineered that the rest of it could be turned to splinters and it would still find a way to fly on unless one of its vital organs was torched. Gustov needed to get closer. His top speed was virtually the same as that of his enemy, but the Rumpler couldn't reach full tilt as it jigged and jagged across the top of Metz's slate shingles. Gustov could catch him only if he stayed high enough to fly straight and fast. Then, when the moment was right and he was directly on top of the man, he'd end it abruptly with a blast from both guns. It would be a pity if Miss Jantz were riding in the observer's seat.

He pushed the throttle as full and fast and hard as he was able. Seconds later, he hurtled toward the point of intersection at almost two hundred kilometers an hour, a speed he had reached before only in his dreams.

****

Ellenor knew she would miss the fourth and final target. Too many buildings flashed by. The plane jostled and jolted to avoid them, shaking her apart. Her guts felt stuck to her lungs.

The bullets that riddled their wing could strike her dead at any moment. She desperately wanted to twist around and look for the plane that chased them, terrified of it, but she couldn't afford to glance away from her target. Her hand shook so violently that the release lever rattled against its housing no matter how tightly she gripped it. She made a high-pitched sound every time she exhaled, bordering on hyperventilation, but she kept her gaze bolted to that single spot on the ground. It got closer, larger.

She pulled the lever and immediately recognized her mistake.

"No!" She clutched the side of the plane and stared at the ground behind them.

The bomb fell too early. Its steel fins angled it

downward and gave it a stabilizing spin. It landed thirty yards from the great wheeled gun, blossoming into a bouquet of flames that did not touch their target.

She missed.

In front of her, Alec shook his head.

Ellenor was about to lean toward him and make a stupid and useless apology, but then the plane whipped forcefully to the left, throwing her into the sidewall and knocking the last of the breath from her body.

Anger and fear washed over her, lining her goggles with tears.

****

Alec saw the German gaining on them. In seconds the man would be close enough to fire. Hildegard could withstand only so much punishment before she fractured, her wooden structure collapsing and sending them to the ground.

The fourth ack-ack had survived. Shit. Nothing could be done about that now. They'd had a damn good run of luck; it was a miracle they'd gotten three of them. Hopefully he and Ellenor had done enough damage that the Frenchies could manage to avoid getting themselves killed in action when they arrived just before dawn to annihilate the factory. Now all that remained undone was escape.

Escape, though, was not to be had. He tried it all, every crafty bit of dancing he could coax from his crate, but the German was too fast and too light in the air.

Alec pulled back on the control wheel, pointing the nose straight at heaven, and then faded to the left and down again, trying in vain to shake the Hun from his tail.

Too late. The bastard arrived and opened fire.

Alec flew through a hailstorm of lead. A strut took a slug and cracked. A piece of laminated wood the size of his arm broke free of the lower-right wing and fluttered like a tossed playing card. The engine took two hits—*ping! ping!*—but amazingly keep churning. Alec did his best to dodge most of the barrage. A lesser pilot would have absorbed so much lead that he would have snapped in half right then and there. Alec bent and twisted his crate in ways it had never moved before, but the iron-hard truth of the matter was that Hildegard was wounded and nearly out of tricks.

Nearly.

Alec knew he and Ellenor had one and only one advantage. They could shoot backwards.

He turned his head and shouted at Ellenor to use the gunner's mounted weapon. She didn't hear him.

"Ellenor!"

The wind devoured his words. The German ripped off another twenty rounds and then hurtled by, close enough that Alec could identify his plane, even in the dark. It was a Fokker *Dreidecker*, a devil with three sets of wings.

"*Ellenor!*"

****

Ellenor leaned forward as much as she possibly could and screamed: "*What?*"

"*Shoot that fucker!*"

Shoot him? Her eyes went to the machine gun mounted on the ring that encircled her seat. What had Alec called it? A para-something. He'd shown her how to unlock it so that it could be rolled out of the way as she worked. Was he now expecting her to fire the damn thing?

In her mounting hysteria, she almost laughed aloud. But if she just sat here, paralyzed now that her last bomb had dropped without effect, she would die, and so would Alec, and that was unacceptable.

As Alec hooked the plane into an upward, right-leaning arc, Ellenor freed the gun as he'd taught her. The weapon instantly rolled along its track in the direction their momentum pushed it. She caught it with trembling hands, then leaned into it, holding it like she'd held the rifle she borrowed from Father's cabinet whenever she visited her hives. She'd used that old bolt-action Mannlicher to scare off foxes and a pair of curious wolves, and of course she'd almost killed Alec with it, and now she repeated what it had taught her: put the stock against the shoulder and sight along the barrel. She remembered to release the safety and chamber the first round.

She peered through the sight and into the swirling chaos of the night.

Everything moved: the plane, the sky, the ground. Nothing was stable anymore. The enemy plane flashed by.

Ellenor pulled the trigger.

The recoil ripped the weapon from her hand. The string of bullets burned tiny red slashes in the dark. She tried to regain control, but Alec was swooping maniacally to dodge the German, who was sending expert bursts at them every twenty seconds. Ellenor, struggling against vertigo, could barely keep the gun braced against her shoulder; she had little chance of hitting a moving target. Tears trapped in her goggles made it nearly impossible to see.

She clamped down on the trigger and didn't let go.

****

Gustov coolly nudged his stick and tipped the Fokker sideways to avoid the river of crimson-coated bullets suddenly pouring at him from the gunner's seat. He realized that it was most likely Ellenor Jantz at the other end of that barrage, which was so spectacular a notion that Gustov couldn't help but shake his head in admiration. He should have met her under different circumstances, at an opera in Monte Carlo, perhaps, or at an equestrian event in Prague. Now he was going to be forced to kill her, which saddened him in an honest and almost boyish way. Innocents had died every day since July of 1914, but one more seemed too much. Her bullets washed the night air without ever endangering him. She had no idea what she was doing; the machine gun was too much for her. That made it even sadder.

For a brief moment, Gustov allowed himself a fantasy: a single shot into the Englander's skull, the pilotless Rumpler gliding mostly safely to the ground, Miss Jantz surviving the crash…

He sighed.

The Rumpler continued evasive maneuvers, now well away from the outskirts of Metz and crisscrossing the sky while attempting to take on altitude. Obviously the Englander planned to use the darkness to escape, so it was imperative that Gustov stay on top of him. Pursuit became a circus of twists, feints, and darting turns that tested Gustov's skill at the stick. Lining up another shot was far from easy, especially with bullets flying back at him from the inexperienced but determined gunner. Gustov danced through them.

He fired in return.

He sent a precise line of lead into the Rumpler's

undercarriage, emptying his first of two ammo drums. Though he couldn't gauge the damage in the dark, he assumed he'd chiseled away much of the landing apparatus. It wasn't a direct hit, but that's how you brought down one of these big bombers—you bled it to death with a thousand razor cuts.

Gustov cleared his mind and let instinct work the controls. He wove through Miss Jantz's bullets and forgot who she was so that he could get on with this business of killing her. In this war, there could be no opera in Monte Carlo or any kind of nice ending at all.

****

Alec ran out of options. The goddamn Hun on his ass was capable of witchcraft at the stick. No matter what Alec tried—from the classic cutbacks taught by the masters to the gambits of a lunatic—the German countered him. Ellenor's constant *rat-a-tat* kept the man at bay, but every minute or so he lunged forward and placed another surgical stitch into Hildegard's wings. The beautiful old bird would not last much longer. Alec needed another option.

Should he land? He considered the outcome. Prisoners of war were treated humanely, especially if they were officers and certainly if they were women. Alec would spend the rest of the war in confinement. Could he do that? Of course he could; the men of the Corbin-Dawes line might be bourgeois nobodies, but they had spine. But he would more than likely never see Ellenor again. They'd be separated. Even if they both survived incarceration, he would lose her forever. At least landing would save her life.

And that was how he decided to set Hildegard down and surrender.

He reduced speed, leveled out, sent the signal he was giving up. Trusting that the German was a man of honor, Alec resisted the urge to fight until his wings were shredded, choosing to provide Ellenor a chance at a life beyond tonight. He would face repercussions for what he'd done, and so would she. But he trusted she'd come out on the other side in one piece, and she'd look back on this and think kindly of him for making the wise choice for once in his life. Sarah, too, would be thankful.

He removed his goggles and felt the wind against his cheeks one last time. Whatever they did to him in the coming weeks or years, they would never let him fly again.

****

Gustov was about to pulverize the Rumpler when it suddenly went limp. The Englander slowed, cruising at a mere hundred kilometers an hour—and now down to eighty. The man presented a target that even a wet rookie couldn't have missed.

"He's white-flagging it," Gustov realized.

The relief that flooded his chest surprised him. Miss Jantz would not die today. Gustov released the trigger. A defeated opponent was yielding the field, and Gustov would nobly accept. He relaxed, nodded to himself, and tucked in directly behind the Englander. The feeling of satisfaction was more potent than he'd anticipated. This was a fight that would make him famous. He'd hunted down a stolen aircraft, beaten the thief in the air, and run the wounded plane to ground to be repaired and sent aloft for the Fatherland again. The story would write itself on the front page of the papers.

What would he say to Ellenor Jantz?

What would she say to *him*?

He rolled his eyes at himself. Fool. More important things awaited: accolades, toasts, a good night's sleep. Flexing the fingers that had turned to granite around the stick, he followed the Englander toward the ground.

****

"*What the hell are you doing?*" Ellenor shouted.

"Saving your arse, thank you very much."

"He'll kill us!"

"Little chance of that, actually. Fairly certain our chap's a man of the code."

Ellenor, scowling, looked back. The German plane was only forty yards behind them, framed against the stars.

Could she simply give up?

They'd been through so much. And what had happened between them a few hours ago was something worth defending. Ellenor needed to see where they would go next, what they'd accomplish together, what this handsome daredevil would say when he realized he loved her. But the only way to discover any of that was to eliminate the German plane, which meant shooting it down.

The machine gun had proven impossible to control. Every time she'd held the trigger down, the damn thing sent tremors into her upper body and ruined her otherwise accurate aim. Using a fully automatic gun required either training or luck, both of which were in short supply. Ellenor knew she had almost no chance of putting all of those shots into the German who chased them.

"I don't need to hit him with a hundred bullets," she said to herself. She needed only one.

She leaned down gently, cheek against the weapon's smooth steel. If she touched the trigger lightly, just a single stroke, she could release a round without having her bones jarred to powder by the fiendish recoil.

Their plane continued its descent. The German mirrored them.

Ellenor closed one eye.

She could not see the pilot directly, but she knew his approximate position. The propeller made a perfect circle; she aimed at the top of its arc. Her papa had taught her to shoot varmints that came to snatch the chickens, and she recalled his lessons about sight picture and center mass. Ellenor had killed more than one opossum and raccoon, and they were tiny creatures—the propeller's circle was at least eight feet across. Behind it was the engine, and behind *that* was the pilot who was bringing them down.

The wind swirled her hair. The stars looked on.

Ellenor fired.

****

Gustov was checking his gauges to ensure a proper touch-down when his prop exploded.

Something struck the blade. The wood split. Then, almost instantly, its own centrifugal force obliterated it. Fragments and jagged bits showered him.

He swore and tugged the stick. He lost almost all his forward speed, the engine still humming but the entire propeller gone, part of it lodged like a spear head in one of the wings.

The Fokker glided.

Gustov fought back. He scooped the nose into position, slapped his hand to the gun, and seared off the remains of his ammo drum. Tracers peppered the air all around the fleeing Rumpler. Gustov *willed* the slugs toward their target, biting down on his teeth in anger, but his bus had already drifted too far, like a powerless swimmer against the tide.

He watched in horror as the Englander took on new speed and climbed straight up.

"Shit!" He slammed the ball of his fist against the cockpit, again and again. Nothing could be done. Just like that, it was over.

Gustov shut off the engine and let the Fokker float wherever the hell physics wanted it to go. He kept it on a stable path, unable to do anything but make sure he landed with his wheels right-side down.

With the motor silent, everything was very quiet as he fell.

He looked up, thinking no thoughts at all, watching Ellenor Jantz and the Englander disappear.

Chapter Twenty-Seven

When Hildegard reached ten thousand feet, Alec finally realized what had happened.

He laughed. That sound was part surprise and part relief at being free and alive. His body still buzzed, and he was a little bit inebriated from being shot at repeatedly and surviving. His head ached; he struggled with disbelief. He owed the victory not to his own skill, but to the woman in the seat behind him.

He reached a hand over his shoulder.

Ellenor found it immediately. He squeezed her fingers: *Damn brilliant work, old girl.*

She squeezed back.

Alec wanted nothing more than to land, spin around, and embrace her. He would kiss her with the full force of his emotions, the good and bad alike, and to hell with the rest of the world and its petty dip-shit bickering. But it was still foreign territory down there. Monsters still lurked. He could not risk putting down.

A small part of him actually felt bad for the German, who'd been caught by surprise in the middle of what he assumed was a truce. Had Ellenor violated an unspoken rule of warfare that would one day come back and demand some kind of karmic recompense? Perhaps. But not today.

He laughed again. Strapped to his seat, there was nothing else he could do.

The wind blew from the northwest, guiding them naturally southeast. Alec settled Hildegard into a steady rhythm in that direction, worrying about her injuries but unable to assess them in the dark. Liberated from her payload, she flew lighter. Still, her dual tanks would be nearly depleted by the time dawn arrived. Until then, Alec would ferry them across Germany, keeping the western Front on his right, reaching for whatever waited beyond.

****

Ellenor reclined in the observer's seat, wrapped in blankets and scarves. Only her eyes were visible, wide open behind her goggles, staring into the lightless morning sky. She thought of dandelions and *bashert* and the way the German's propeller had burst like a sand dollar struck by a fist. She thought of Alec's hands on her bare back and of the taste of his lips. She thought of things she'd never seen before, the unknown town where they would eat their next meal.

Most of all she thought of flying.

"May it never end," she whispered, and closed her eyes.

****

Just before sunrise, a late-model Adler bearing the Air Service insignia murmured to a stop in front of a telegraph station five kilometers east of Metz. Two men climbed from the car. The driver was like drivers everywhere: blunt and colorless and in need of a better-fitting tunic. The passenger wore ankle boots, clean puttees, and a single-breasted coat with officer's marks on the arms. His hair was longer than regulation, which indicated his assigned post was so removed from the action that no one gave a damn how he looked. He yawned and stretched and seemed like a man who had not yet eaten his breakfast or smoked his first pipe of the day.

Gustov sat in the grass, cross-legged, and watched them.

He'd already worked through the possibilities. In the hours while he'd waited to be picked up after sending his report with the help of a bleary-eyed radio man, he had time to sort it out. He assumed one of two fates awaited him. They would reassign him, or they would simply drive him back to his squadron and let him resume his duties. Both options came with a severe reprimand, as he'd not only managed to let a bomber be stolen out from under him, but he'd permitted that very plane to destroy German property, kill German troops, and then fly away unpunished. If Gustov's family weren't politically and fiscally connected to so many people with important-sounding names, he might have ended up demoted to gunner or—far worse— transferred to the infantry.

He stood up.

The officer approached. In the anemic light from an electrical bulb above the door of the telegraph station, Gustov noted the man's rank of major. Reluctantly, Gustov saluted.

The major returned the greeting. "Captain Voss, I assume?"

"That is correct, sir."

"Shot down, I hear."

"Yes, sir."

"A pity. Your aircraft?"

"Salvageable."

"Good." The major's demeanor changed. He

slouched a bit, as if tired of the formalities so early in the morning. "My name is Baumann. To be entirely honest with you, Voss, the lieutenant-general who dispatched me told me nothing at all about your mission, and frankly I don't care to know. But I've been ordered to bring you to Berlin. Is that acceptable?"

Berlin? Gustov recalculated. Apparently he had more than two possible fates. He hadn't been to the capital since before the war, and to be summoned there now was unusual, to say the least. Revealing none of this to Baumann, he nodded. "Of course, sir."

"Glad to hear it." The major looked relieved; perhaps he'd been expecting resistance. "It's a considerable drive, so if you don't mind, I'd like to get a bite of food first and a pot of coffee, the blacker the better. Can you recommend a suitable eatery in Metz?"

Gustov assured him that he knew of such a place, and then followed the man to the waiting car. Berlin could mean many things, both good and bad. The city could immortalize you or turn you to a pillar of salt at a glance. Removing his hat, Gustov settled into the rear seat and stared from the window while the driver got them moving toward town.

Without realizing it, his eyes strayed to the southeast.

Epilogue

One hundred and twenty-five miles from Metz, on the banks of the High Rhine, three nations collide. Germany and France grind against each other as they have for years. Beyond the river that runs scarlet with their soldiers' blood, Switzerland abides, beholden to none. The Swiss border city of Basel, defiantly neutral, offers solace to anyone weary of war.

Though the summer morning is only an hour old, Kjell has been awake for quite some time, having fired his ovens while others slept. His bakery has persevered while his rivals have lost business during these times of privation and mindful spending, primarily because he keeps to the basics of bread and croissants and doesn't bother with unnecessary treats. Artfully rendered *macarons* and creamy *religieuse* doomed many of his peers. Kjell is sweeping up a flour spill near the window when he sees the man and woman approach.

They hold hands. He is tall and yellow-haired and wearing horseman's boots. She's clad in a uniform reminiscent of the military. Kjell has never seen anything like her. Her dark hair falls over her shoulders instead of being pinned away. Her jacket is unbuttoned, revealing the curve of her breasts beneath her sweater.

Kjell knows all his customers, but he does not know them. When they enter his shop, he carefully sets his broom aside.

****

"I don't know why you've brought me here if we have no money," Ellenor says.

"Who says we have no money?"

She gives him a glance as they observe the array of baked goods. "You need to shave."

"I'm told that some women find this look attractive."

"Do these women live in caves?"

He smirks. "Tart."

She bumps him with her hip. "You haven't answered my question."

Alec withdraws a roll of Swiss *francs*.

"Where on earth did you get that?"

"Sarah. She insisted on looking after me."

"How much is it?"

"Enough for two days."

"Two days? And what do we do after that? On day number three? And day four?"

"Find work, I suppose."

"Find work doing what?"

"I don't know. Do you think anyone around here needs to hire a handsome pilot and a beautiful machine-gunner?"

Ellenor slides her hand into the crook of his elbow. Smiling, she returns her attention to the loaves, filling herself with their scent. Nothing seems to matter at the moment but choosing the right one. Without looking away from the sourdoughs and pumpernickels and ryes, she says, "Will we live here in Basel?"

A few seconds pass before he replies. "Is that what you want?"

"For a while."

"And when a while is over?"

Ellenor has narrowed it down to the yeast rolls and the rye with warm butter. "I think I'd like to see my bees again."

"I'm sure there are beekeepers in Switzerland."

"That one," she says, pointing to the loaf of rye.

On the other side of the counter, the baker nods and fetches a square of newsprint and a length of twine.

She watches the man work. "Will we ever know if the French made it through?"

"I'm sure they did. I never met a Frenchman who wasn't as tenacious as a terrier."

"A nucleus won't be cheap, you know."

"Nucleus?"

"That's what you call the queen and a small amount of bees you buy from a beekeeper in order to raise your own colony. And we'll need at least two of them to get started, just to be sure. We'll have to hurry, because the hives need time to build up their honey stores before winter."

"What do you say we worry about getting a roof over our heads first, and *then* we'll look into acquiring a few bees?"

Ellenor accepts the wrapped bread and looks up at Alec. "I warn you that my domestic skills are unrefined."

"How's your sharpshooting?"

She smiles and puts one arm around his neck. "Better than average."

Alec buries his hands in her hair, pulls her onto her toes, and kisses her.

The baker, embarrassed, hurries back to his broom.

A word about the author...

Lance Hawvermale published his first books under the pseudonym of Erin O'Rourke. Since then, his poetry and fiction have garnered numerous awards.

Hawvermale is an alumnus of AmeriCorps. He has worked as a college professor, an editor, and a youth counselor. He lives in Texas with his family and their honey bees.

Visit his website at:
www.lancehawvermale.com